DANNY ORLIS
AND
JOHNNY'S
NEW LIFE

DANNY ORLIS

AND

JOHNNY'S NEW LIFE

BERNARD PALMER

Aneko Press Youth

www.anekopress.com

Aneko Press, Life Sentence Publishing, and our logos are trademarks of Life Sentence Publishing, Inc.
203 E. Birch Street
P.O. Box 652
Abbotsford, WI 54405

JUVENILE FICTION / Religious / Christian / Action & Adventure

Paperback ISBN: 979-8-88936-054-4

eBook ISBN: 979-8-88936-055-1

10 9 8 7 6 5 4 3 2 1

Available where books are sold

CONTENTS

CHAPTER 1

THE SEARCH

Fall was always the most pleasant time of the year in Fairview, Minnesota. The days were warm and the nights crisp and cool. The woods around town were splashed with color. But the Davis triplets didn't notice the beauty of the turning leaves or the warmth of the afternoons. They were too busy trying to get readjusted to their studies after their exciting summer. They came home from school each afternoon, loaded down with books.

Danny Orlis was sitting in the living room alone when DeeDee and Doug came in.

He looked up. "Well, how did school go today?" DeeDee, who was on her way to her room, didn't hear him, but Doug dropped his books on the table with a resounding thud and turned.

"Hi, Danny."

"Getting back into the harness at school?" Danny asked.

"I guess so."

"You don't sound very excited about it."

"What's there to get excited about? It's the same old grind. We have to study in school all day and bring home a half a ton of books for homework every night."

"I feel sorry for you, Doug. Another minute and you'll have me crying because you're so abused."

There was a brief moment of silence. Doug moved across the room and sat down. It was good to be back in Fairview, sitting across the room from Danny and talking about school. Being in Texas had been fun, but now Fairview was home, and Danny and Kay were like Mother and Dad would have been. He had never realized that quite as much as he did at that minute.

"I saw Johnny Larson on the street today," he began after a time. "What are the police going to do about him, anyway?"

Thoughtfully, Danny folded his newspaper. "They're going to have his trial one of these days. I don't know for sure just when it's going to be."

Doug scooted down in the chair until his head was lower than the back of it. His legs were sprawled grotesquely. "We sure thought a lot about him when we were down on the ranch. Do you think they'll put him in jail, or what?"

Danny tugged at the lobe of his ear. "I couldn't say what they'll do to him. He'll be punished. I know that much, but the judge is the one who'll have to decide what the punishment will be and for how long."

Doug pulled himself erect, his gaze seeking Danny's. "I sure wouldn't want to trade places with him," he said. "When I saw him today, he looked sad. I don't think he's smiled for a year."

"I don't suppose he has," Danny said. "You know, Doug, it would be a terrible thing to be responsible for the death of one of your friends."

"That's what Del and I were saying. And then having to be arrested and tried would make it a lot worse."

Danny folded the newspaper without speaking.

After a time, Doug continued the conversation. "Johnny sure got himself into a jam by toying with sin, didn't he?"

"That sort of thing happens to everybody who tries to live apart from God," Danny said. "I don't mean that every person who isn't a Christian is going to get into trouble with the law, or anything like that. What I mean is that sin is a dead end and can only cause trouble and heartbreak."

Doug got slowly to his feet. "It sure makes a guy want to live for Christ, doesn't it?"

Doug knew well enough what Johnny would say if he or anyone else asked for advice about drinking or running with a rough crowd. He had never talked with the older boy about it, but he had seen the remorse in his eyes. He knew that he would give anything in the world if he could only live over that night when Fritz McCloud had been killed and do differently.

Danny was the one who changed the subject. "Where's Del? Didn't he come home with you and DeeDee?"

"You might guess." Scorn crept into Doug's voice. "He had to go out and see if he could find that deer of his."

Danny laid aside the paper and stood. "I think I'll go out and see him. Which direction did he go?"

"Down by the lake." Doug paused. "Think he'll find Jumper?"

"I wouldn't know for sure, but I wouldn't be surprised."

Danny crossed the farmyard and went into the woods in the direction of the lake. If Del had left more than a few minutes ago it would have been impossible for Danny to locate him in the thick woods. As it was, however, he had only been gone five or ten minutes. That didn't give him time enough to get far.

Danny hadn't covered more than three hundred yards or so into the forest before he heard Del somewhere ahead. "Del!" he called out. "Del! Wait up!"

"Over here, Danny!" Disappointment clouded Del's eyes.

"What's the matter? Aren't you glad to see me?" Danny asked him.

"Sure I am, but I thought maybe you were–" His voice seemed to run out of power to get past his lips. He stopped abruptly and it was a minute or so before he could speak again. "Have you seen him this summer, Danny?" he asked, at last.

Danny knew he was talking about the young deer but pretended that he didn't. "Have I seen whom?"

"Jumper. Have you seen him around the place since we left for Texas?"

The pilot nodded. "Now that you mention it, we saw him around every once in a while after you kids left for Texas."

"Have you seen him lately?" Del wanted to know.

Danny saw the concern in the boy's eyes and was sorry he had even planned on teasing him. His expression changed. "No, I haven't seen him for the last month or so."

Del's fear increased. "Are–are you sure?"

"I'm positive about it, Del. Kay and I both have looked around for him every time we've gone outside. It's been several weeks since either of us saw him."

That seemed to be more of a blow than Del could bear. The light in his dark eyes faded and he seemed to grow numb and wooden. "Do–do you think some hunters killed him, Danny?" he asked. "The way they killed his mother?"

The creases in Danny's forehead deepened. "I

honestly can't tell you about that, Del, because I don't know one way or the other."

The boy flinched as though Danny had struck him in the face.

"But," the pilot hastened to add, "I can't recall that there's been any evidence around here that anyone has been poaching on our place this summer. And besides, a poacher would want a bigger pile of meat than Jumper represents. They wouldn't want to risk getting caught for an animal his size."

Still, Del was far from satisfied that some illegal hunter hadn't killed the little deer. "The way I look at it," he said, voicing his concern, "if something hasn't happened to him, I ought to be able to find him. I'm sure he wouldn't have wandered away. He was too tame for that."

They were still standing there, motionless, when the bell sounded, calling them to dinner. Del started on, but Danny stopped him.

"Don't you think we ought to go in and eat now?" he asked gently.

"I want to look for Jumper while it's still light."

"I think we had better go in and eat now," Danny continued. "It will probably take quite a while for us to find Jumper. The chances are we wouldn't be able to locate him tonight, no matter how long we stayed out here looking for him."

Their gaze met.

"I've got to find out what happened to him," Del said, his voice taut with emotion. "I've just got to!"

Danny put an arm over the boy's shoulder affectionately. "We'd better go back to the house now so Kay doesn't worry, but I'll tell you what we'll do. Tomorrow, as soon as the bus comes home, we'll all go out and look for him."

Del turned, because he could think of nothing else to do, and shuffled back to the house with Danny. He didn't know why he was going to sit down at the table. He sure wasn't hungry.

Doug was already at the table, waiting impatiently. "We thought you were never coming. Snap it up, will you? We're about starved!"

Del eyed him without speaking. He didn't feel like talking to anybody. And especially to Doug. He would be the last one who could understand how he felt about not being able to find Jumper. All Doug cared about was football.

Del was right about Doug. At least at the dinner table that night all he could talk about was the football coach and the plays they were learning and the games they were going to play.

"And I think I've got a chance of making the team. Isn't that great?"

Del scowled. "Yeah, big deal!"

"You wouldn't talk that way if you'd just go out for football once. You'd find out how much fun it is."

Del looked up, eyes squinting narrowly.

"Really, you ought to try out, Del. All the guys have been asking about you."

Del knew well enough why Doug wanted to get him out for football. He wanted to show him up again the way he had during basketball season. Well, he could talk all he wanted to. He wasn't going to get *him* out for football! That was all there was to it!

As soon as they finished eating, Danny got the Bible, read a chapter, and asked for prayer requests.

"I'd like to have you pray that I'll find Jumper alive," Del said quickly.

Doug laughed. "Somebody's probably got his head mounted and hanging on the wall in his living room."

"Doug!" Danny spoke sternly. "That's not being very kind."

Doug's temper flashed. "I was just kidding. What's the matter? Can't he take a little joke?"

Danny turned to face him. "Let's hear no more of that kind of talk. OK?"

Doug fell silent.

When they had finished praying that Jumper would be found, DeeDee raised her head, revealing the tears that glistened in her eyes. "I'll go out with you tomorrow after school and help you look for Jumper."

"So will I," Kay put in.

"I already told Del I'd help," Danny said.

Color tinged Doug's cheeks. "I've got to go out for football," he muttered defensively.

Danny was slow in speaking. "I know you'd hate to think that Jumper would forget you and go somewhere else, Del," he said, choosing his words with care. "But you've got to remember that he's a wild animal and his instinct for the wilds is much greater than any feeling he might have had for you. I honestly don't think anything has happened to him. I think he's simply drifted deeper into the forest and doesn't get over this way anymore– Or at least he hasn't for the last month or so."

"I sure hope you're right." A pale grin flickered briefly. "I'd feel a lot better just knowing that he's still alive – even if he wouldn't come over here anymore."

"I know just how you feel," Kay said.

* * *

The next two or three days they searched for Jumper carefully but could find no trace of him. It began to look as though Danny was actually right and that they wouldn't see Jumper again. Saturday came and Del prepared to go out quite early in the morning to continue his search. DeeDee saw him head for the door alone.

"Is anyone going with you, Del?" she asked.

He shook his head. "Nope. I'm going alone."

"I told you I've got to memorize the plays the coach gave us," Doug retorted defensively. "Besides, you're not going to find Jumper. You'd just as well give up."

9

"That's what you think."

That seemed to make up DeeDee's mind for her. "Wait a minute. I'll go with you."

Ordinarily Del didn't think much of having their sister along, but this particular morning he was glad for her company. "Sure thing." He opened the door. "I want to go out to the barn first. I'll meet you at the gate."

A few minutes later they were making their way down the narrow path to the water's edge.

"I sure am glad you came along, DeeDee," he told her.

She glanced at him quickly. Del could be nice when he wanted to be, even if he was her brother. "I think Doug is wrong, Del. We are going to find Jumper."

His smile came again. It was good having someone else to share his opinion that they were going to find Jumper alive. It seemed to give him strength.

DeeDee and Del fell silent. They walked down to the lake and made their way quietly along the shore. DeeDee was thinking about the horses that would soon be arriving from Texas.

"When I think about them, Del," she said, "I get so excited I can hardly wait for them to get here. Isn't it going to be fun to have horses to ride anywhere we want to go?"

Her brother's expression did not change, and, when he spoke, his voice was heavy and lifeless. He sounded as though he could never be excited about anything again. "I guess I was excited about getting a horse at first but, to tell you the truth, DeeDee, I don't much care whether they ever get here or not."

"Del!" his sister exclaimed. "Don't say such a terrible thing!"

There was a brief silence.

Before either of them could speak again, there was a slight noise in the brush along the lakeshore some thirty yards or so ahead of them. They stopped suddenly.

"Del!" DeeDee cried. "Look!"

There along the water's edge stood a half-grown deer.

"Jumper!" DeeDee said under her breath. "It's Jumper!"

CHAPTER 2

CONFLICTING INTERESTS

For the space of half a minute or more, neither Del nor DeeDee moved. They stared at the half-grown deer, scarcely daring to breathe for fear they would startle him.

They were not alone in their surprise and uncertainty. Jumper was eyeing them just as questioningly. He cocked his head to one side and took a hesitant half step forward. Natural caution kept him from approaching boldly. While they waited, he paused, undecided whether those figures that were somehow familiar were friend or enemy. From somewhere in the back of his alert young mind he seemed to sense that they were not to be feared. Yet, there was the natural fear of man, and his protective instinct signaled danger and distrust. But these humans made no suspicious move. There was nothing about them that caused him to be alarmed. Curious, he walked forward with quick, dainty steps. Del was certain that Jumper remembered and was going to approach them.

Then the deer stopped. Fear and curiosity mingled in his luminous brown eyes.

"Stay here a minute," Del whispered softly to his sister. "Maybe I can get close to him if I'm alone."

DeeDee frowned but did as she was told. Del inched forward, hand extended in a friendly, reassuring way.

At the first move Jumper moved to one side. He had not been frightened enough to dash away, but it was obvious that he was alarmed. Every fiber in the deer's being was tense. His legs were taut, ready to spring into action. His head was up, eyes fixed and nostrils flaring.

Del stopped where he was and remained motionless.

When Del did not move again, the deer relaxed slightly. Neither his head nor his eyes moved, but the bowstring tautness of his body seemed to ease and the wild fright began to soften.

Del took another slow, cautious step.

"Jumper!" His voice was scarcely above a whisper. "Jumper!"

The deer's lithe body jerked into tense, expectant readiness again. His eyes rolled in fear of this strange being that was approaching him and making strange noises. Del saw what was about to happen and stopped, but he was too late. Jumper whirled and bounded away.

The boy stared after him miserably. "He's gone!" he half-whispered. "He doesn't remember me!"

"You shouldn't feel bad about that, Del," DeeDee told him. "A couple of minutes ago we were wondering if he was alive or not. Now we know that he is. Don't forget that."

A faint smile crept to the boy's lips. "You're right about that. We know that Jumper's all right. And that means a lot to me."

DeeDee's face brightened. "That's what I was thinking. He may not remember you, but at least we know that he's alive and that the poachers didn't get him this summer. That ought to make you feel good."

"It does," he repeated.

Still, Del's eyes were sad, and he didn't talk much as they made their way back to the farmhouse where they lived with Danny and Kay. DeeDee continued to chatter excitedly about the horses Uncle Clarence had promised to ship to them from the Circle R ranch in Texas and wondered aloud about how long it would be until the beautiful saddle ponies would get to Fairview. Del answered her questions when he couldn't get out of it, but it was obvious that he scarcely heard what she was saying.

"You don't even care whether Uncle Clarence sends the horses to us, Del," she retorted.

"Sure I do."

"You don't act much like it. To tell you the truth, if

I were him, I don't think I'd even send you a horse," she exclaimed in exasperation.

He paused, facing her. "Why? What'd I do now?"

"That's just it. You haven't done anything. I talk to you about the horses, and all you do is grunt and say that it's going to be nice when they get here. You don't act as though it matters to you one way or the other about the saddle horses."

"What do you want me to do?" His voice revealed his irritation. "Turn handsprings? I'm glad Uncle Clarence is sending the horses up to us. I'm glad we're going to be able to ride anywhere we want to. I think it's wonderful that we've got an Uncle like him. There! Does that satisfy you?"

Her black eyes flamed. "You make me so mad!"

Del managed a little grin. "I'm sorry, DeeDee. I'm really happy about the horses Uncle Clarence gave to us, and I think he's the greatest uncle anyone ever had." His smile died. "But I am upset about Jumper not remembering me. I've been trying to figure out how to get him tamed again, that's all."

DeeDee's expression softened. "I'll help you, Del, if there's anything I can do."

* * *

Doug Davis didn't spend a great deal of time around the farmhouse after school and football started. He liked the game as well as he did basketball but wasn't sure that he could play well enough to make the team.

"When is the coach going to cut the squad, anyway?" he asked Johnny Larson's younger brother, Larry.

"I don't know for sure, but it shouldn't be too long." Larry picked up a stone and quickly threw it across the street with a swift, sure movement. "Why? You aren't afraid of getting weeded out, are you?"

Doug hesitated. He wasn't sure that he would survive the cut. That was what bothered him so much. "I'll feel a lot better when it's over, if I'm still on the squad."

"Oh, you don't have anything to worry about. You'll make it all right."

Doug was not so sure. He had seen Larry and some of the other fellows out for practice. They were good!

"What about Del?" Larry asked suddenly. "Is he going out for football this year?"

"Del?" Doug echoed. "You won't catch him out for football. He hasn't got time. He's got to fool around trying to tame a deer or catch a rabbit in some kind of a live trap he and Danny rigged up."

"That's too bad. He can really move when he wants to."

"That's the trouble," Doug said. "He simply doesn't want to."

That was probably as accurate an appraisal of Del as anyone had ever made. He didn't want to go out for sports. Del had to admit that he was proud of the fact that Doug was good at sports, yet he couldn't help feeling envious when the kids at school kept talking about Doug and how he was sure to be as much a star on the football field as he was at basketball. Kids Del scarcely knew came up to him and wanted to know why he wasn't out for the team.

"That brother of yours is sure good," one ninth grader said. "The coach told some of us that he might make the best quarterback Fairview has ever had by the time he gets into high school."

Del colored. "That's fine. That's great."

The boy's smile teased the corners of his mouth. "How come you aren't out for football, Del?"

He knew he was flushing crimson. "I just happen to have something better to do with my time than play football."

"Boy, if I were in your place, I'd sure be out for the team. I wouldn't let my brother get ahead of me. I can tell you that much."

Del did not answer. It wasn't his fault that he wasn't any good at sports. Why did they have to think that he could do as well as Doug did in everything? Why couldn't they leave him alone?

And it wasn't only the boys who were talking. Every now and then he overheard some girls talking about Doug and how good he was on the football field. Invariably, when they were talking about Doug, Del would hear his name, too. Sometimes they talked about what a poor sport he was or laid his lack of interest in football to no school spirit. Other times he didn't hear what they were saying, but it really didn't matter. The tone in their voices revealed plainly enough the disgust they had for him.

Del tried to pretend as though he didn't care what anybody said; that he wasn't interested in football or their opinion of him, but it *did* hurt – deeply. Every time it happened a knife plunged into his heart.

Things were bad enough for him during that football season, as bad as they had been during basketball the winter before. But they would have been far worse had he not had Jumper to think about. Every afternoon, as soon as he got home, he went out in the woods looking for the elusive half-grown deer.

Actually Jumper seemed to know he was looking for him and was just as determined not to be seen as Del was determined to find him. Only once did Del get a glimpse of his pet deer, and that time Jumper was so far away Del didn't even try to attract his attention or get close to him. He knew from experience that it would be useless.

After that he didn't so much as catch a glimpse of Jumper again; and, as the days passed, his discouragement began to grow.

Danny had had a lot of experience with wild animals when he was a boy living on Angle Inlet and Del often went to him for advice. Danny always had time for him.

"This isn't anything that ought to get you shaken up, Del," Danny assured him. "You want to remember that Jumper is still a wild animal in spite of the fact that you had him gentle enough to eat out of your hand and walk up to you boldly. You've got to give him time to get used to you, Del. Every natural instinct in the little guy tells him that you represent danger."

"But I don't," the boy protested. "You know I wouldn't do anything to hurt him."

"You and I know that, but Jumper doesn't. You've simply got to find him and gentle him again."

The confidence in Danny's voice seemed to give Del confidence, too. He brightened noticeably. "Do you think I can?"

"I don't think you'll have any trouble at all, Del. He was tame once. You'll be able to tame him again. I'm sure of it."

The boy picked up his fork and toyed with it momentarily, scarcely realizing that he was holding anything in his hand. "If we'd stayed home last summer, Jumper would still be as tame as ever," he said wistfully. "It almost makes me wish we had."

Doug spoke quickly. "If we hadn't gone to Texas, we wouldn't have been able to help Mack Flores and his mother and brothers and sisters."

"That's right," DeeDee put in, eyes gleaming. "And we wouldn't be getting our very own saddle horses, either."

"That reminds me," Danny said, fishing in his pocket for a crumpled envelope. "We got a letter from your Uncle Clarence today. He says we ought to be getting those saddle ponies next week sometime. They've already been shipped from Texas."

In spite of Del's concern for Jumper, neither he nor Doug nor DeeDee were able to sleep at all that night.

CHAPTER 3

CONNIE'S DECISION

The Fairview Clarion had a front-page news story about Johnny Larson's impending trial. It related the story of Fritz McCloud's death in minute detail, going back to his efforts to befriend Johnny and the ironic turn that caused Johnny to be responsible for Fritz' death. According to the news story the trial was to be held the following week.

When Connie McCloud got that issue of the paper at Cedarton Bible Institute she was very disturbed about it. She read it over three or four times, slowly, while each detail drove to the very depths of her being – fiery darts that would torment her until she could get no rest.

Winnie Blair was away when the mail came, but when she got back to their room an hour later, Connie was lying on the bed, crying softly. The paper was lying open on the bedspread beside her.

"Connie!" Winnie cried, rushing to her. "What's the matter? What's wrong?"

Connie could not answer her.

"Did something happen?" Winnie dropped to the bed and put an arm about her best friend's shoulder. "What is it, Connie?"

Connie looked up, tear-blurred eyes seeking Winnie's. She tried to speak, but the words clogged her throat. Silently she handed Winnie the paper.

At a glance, the other girl knew what was wrong. "I'm sorry for you, Connie." Her voice was a little more than a whisper. "Honestly, I am. I had a letter from the folks yesterday telling me about it. It'll probably be quite an ordeal for all of you."

After a time, Connie got control of herself enough to sit up and speak.

"I guess I knew this was going to come up before long, but nobody mentioned it to me and I–I'm just not prepared for it." Her voice broke with a sob.

Winifred tried to comfort her friend, but there was nothing she could say. At such a time words were useless. So, although she knew what was in the newspaper article, she read it over thoughtfully.

"What do you think, Winnie?" Connie asked. "What will they do to Johnny?"

The other girl shook her head.

"I wish I knew." She breathed deeply. "All I know is that Fritz was so well liked it's apt to go very hard for Johnny."

Connie sat up, wiping her eyes. The anger that had gleamed there such a short time before was gone now. "You know, Winnie, right after Fritz was killed all I could think about was getting revenge for his death. We all had been hurt so terribly that I thought the only way I could be happy again was to see Johnny Larson punished severely."

Winifred nodded. "I've heard you say that often enough."

"I thought the only way I would ever be satisfied would be by seeing Johnny Larson put in prison for a long, long time. I had convinced myself that my hatred of him was Christian – that I had a right to see him punished the way we were punished by having Fritz killed."

Winifred Blair waited for her distraught friend to continue.

"I still feel terrible about it," Connie continued, "but in an entirely different way. I feel terrible to think that Johnny is going to have to be punished for what he did."

Her friend's eyes widened. "I didn't think I'd ever hear you say that."

"And I didn't think I'd ever say it. But now I can honestly say that I don't want him to have to go to the reformatory or wherever it is they send fellows for getting drunk and killing someone while they're driving." There was a long, tortured silence. "Right now, I almost wish there wasn't such a law."

"Oh, don't say that," Winnie answered quickly. "We've got to think about the others who might be killed by other drunken drivers unless something is done to put a stop to their driving when they're drunk. The law has to do something to Johnny. There has to be some sort of punishment as an example to others."

Connie got to her feet and walked slowly to the window, where she stood looking out over the campus. It was a long while before she spoke again. "I know Johnny broke the law and that he should have to pay the penalty, but it–" Her voice choked. "I just wish it didn't have to be this way!"

* * *

Jim Morgan did not subscribe to the Fairview weekly newspaper, so he didn't get the account of Johnny Larson's forthcoming trial until Kay Orlis sent him the clipping with her letter. He read it over slowly, almost as slowly and as thoughtfully as Connie had done – but for a slightly different reason.

That trial was one of the things that had made the past summer so rough for Connie McCloud, he thought. She couldn't forget the fact that her brother had been killed by a drunken driver. Nobody in Fairview would let her forget it. She had to relive it in agonizing detail once or twice a week. And sometimes it was even oftener as thoughtless people tried to sympathize by expressing their contempt for

Johnny and voicing their hope that he would get a severe sentence.

Now, with the trial about to be held, things would probably be even worse for Connie. It would start the gossip again and the well-meaning individuals who thought they could help her by talking about Johnny Larson. Jim folded the clipping and returned it to the envelope. It was no wonder that she didn't take part in the activities at school and very often didn't even come down for her meals.

Jim didn't know exactly when he decided that he had to go over and see Connie, nor did he know just why he felt that he had to go. All he knew was that suddenly he felt he had to get in touch with her. Leaving his books untouched on his desk, he got up and went over to the girls' dormitory. The girl at the desk knew whom he wanted to see before he asked her.

"I'll call Connie and ask her to come down," she said.

"Is she in?"

"I think so." The smile was warm and friendly. He went over and sat down. There were magazines on the table near the chair, but he was too concerned to do any reading that particular evening. Almost everyone else was studying and the lounge was nearly deserted. The few who were there weren't paying any attention to him.

It took Connie so long to come down from her room that he was afraid she wasn't going to come.

He was about ready to get up and go back to his own dorm when she came, her face pale and somber.

It made Jim's heart ache just to look at her. At that moment she looked as though she never would be happy again. She tried to smile, but there was a sadness in her eyes that seemed to have no end to it. Connie stopped five or six feet away from him. Her lips parted, but she did not speak.

He got to his feet, suddenly ill at ease. "H-hello, Connie."

Her reply was wooden and far away.

"You–you wanted to see me?" she asked.

He nodded.

There was a long silence.

"I got a letter from Kay this afternoon," he began, "with a clipping from the *Clarion*. It made me realize that I–I had to come over and–and talk to you– That is, if you would talk to me."

The softness came back to her face. "I'd never refuse to talk to you, Jim," she said in a small voice. "You know that." A trace of the old tenderness came back, the tenderness that she had reserved for him, back in the days before Fritz' death had mixed things up and ruined everything. But it was visible only for an instant. The corners of her mouth tightened and her reserve came back. "What did you want to talk to me about?"

He looked about. Strange, how many more kids were in the lounge now. A few minutes ago he had thought it almost empty. Now it seemed that they were milling everywhere.

"Could we find a quiet corner where we could talk?" he asked.

"Couldn't we stay here?"

"Well," he answered reluctantly, "I suppose we can, if you insist; but I'd at least like to find a place where we won't have so many hearing what I've got to say."

Her cheeks flushed.

"I–I'm sorry, Jim. I'm afraid my mind isn't working very well tonight. Let's go over there."

They went to the far corner of the lounge to a couple of chairs that were some distance from any others. Even after they sat down, however, it was some time before Jim could bring himself to say what was burning inside. Connie had to bring it out in the open.

"I think I know what the clipping was about, Jim," she told him quietly.

He cleared his throat. "I suppose you do. I'd forgotten that you get the paper."

"This is one time I almost wish I didn't," she confessed. "Since it came and I read the story about Johnny's trial, I haven't been able to think about anything else."

Jim Morgan nodded understandingly. "I knew it would be that way with you, Connie. That was the big reason I came over to talk with you."

Her smile softened the sting of her words. "There

isn't very much that we can do by talking about it, Jim. It's one of those things that have got to be faced."

"I know." For an instant, his voice was harsh. "I didn't come over here just to talk with you about it. I wanted to tell you that I'm going to be praying for you in a special way from now until after the trial."

Connie McCloud looked up at him quickly. She thought she had full control of herself, but too late she realized that she did not. Her eyes grew wide and her lips trembled. Then, without warning, she burst into tears.

Jim Morgan sat motionless, staring miserably at her. He longed to take her in his arms and comfort her, or try to. When Connie cried it seemed as though there was nothing that anybody could do. She was so distraught and beyond comfort.

"Connie," he said, "is–is there anything I can do? Anything at all?"

She fought to stem the flow of tears. "No!" she blurted with a harshness she did not feel. "There's nothing anybody can do. This is one thing that I've got to work out myself."

She knew she didn't mean that, even as she said it. It wasn't anything she could work out in the first place. She already had proven to herself that she was incapable of working out anything. For a brief, terrified instant all she wanted to do was to jump to her feet and flee to the safety and quiet of her room. But she couldn't do that. Not when Jim had been kind enough to come over and try to help her. Not when he had just said he was praying for her.

Jim wasn't like so many of the others who tried to talk with her about it. He was genuinely concerned. And she knew that he would do anything to help ease the pain.

Her gaze met his, forcibly, and held it.

Jim spoke again, still as anguished and as concerned as before. "I wish there was something I could do to help you."

She dabbed the tears from her eyes with a tissue. "Thank you, Jim." This time all the resentment and confusion were gone from her voice. "I appreciate your coming over tonight more than you'll ever know. But, like I said, this is one of those things that, with the Lord's help, I've got to work out for myself."

His gaze was unwavering, but he looked so dejected. Connie's heart ached for him. Impulsively she reached out her hand.

"I'm sorry, Jim," she murmured. "Honestly, I am."

"So am I." He got to his feet. "I know that you don't care to go with me anymore, Connie. And that's your privilege. But, if you ever need anything or if you'd like someone to talk to or pray with, just give me a ring. OK?"

He would have left, but she stood, too, her eyes imploring him to wait for an explanation.

"It's not at all like you think it is, Jim," she began uncertainly.

His straight young body stiffened. "What do you mean by that?"

Connie lacked the words she wanted to tell him how she felt about him and Fritz' death and Johnny Larson and all of the other things that were such a jumble in her mind.

"I know you think I don't want to go with you anymore because I don't care about you," she began, "but that's not it." She swallowed against the lump in her throat. "I don't have the right to go with you anymore."

He took a deep breath. That wasn't what he had expected to hear her say. "And why don't you have the right to go with me anymore?" he demanded. In spite of himself, anger tinged his voice – anger triggered by a lack of understanding.

Connie caught the tone in his voice and sensed the reason for it. "I can't date you or anyone else because of Fritz' death."

"What does that have to do with it?"

"I can't even think of anything other than serving the Lord," she went on. "I've got to take Fritz' place. I've got to do what God had called him to do." Agony gleamed in her eyes. "Don't you see, Jim? As much as I like you, I can't allow myself to go with you!"

He stared numbly. So that was the reason Connie didn't want to go with him. Somehow, she had gotten the idea that God was looking to her to take Fritz' place in His scheme of things. Jim wasn't exactly sure just what she meant by that. He thought she meant that God was expecting her to witness to the people Fritz would have witnessed to, and do the things for Him that Fritz would have done – like singing in the choir and helping with camp and perhaps even going out on the mission field, if that was where God had called her brother.

The thought didn't make much sense to Jim. She still would have her own Christian responsibilities to take care of. It didn't seem reasonable to him that God would load Fritz' work on Connie as well.

However, Jim felt as though a terrible burden had been lifted from him. He never had seen or heard that Connie was going with anyone else. Yet, he hadn't been able to put that thought out of mind. It seemed the only logical explanation for her sudden refusal to go with him. Just knowing there was some other reason was enough to make him feel a lot better.

Still, that didn't ease Connie's heart, he realized. He knew he could only guess at the turmoil she was experiencing. He wanted to talk with her. He wanted to tell her that God wouldn't expect her to take over a single responsibility that had been Fritz', that He calls each of us to a specific work and that the other members of our families can't pick up those unfinished tasks and do them.

Although Jim Morgan knew that it was best for him to leave, he had to force himself to do so. "Good-bye, Connie," he said softly. "I'll be praying for you."

When he got back to his own room, he dropped to his knees beside the bed and prayed for Connie. He asked God to help her over the next difficult days and to help her get straightened out and know exactly what He would have her to do.

The following day when Jim met Connie on the campus between classes, she smiled and spoke to him. It was only a little thing, but it warmed his entire day.

CHAPTER 4

PATIENCE REWARDED

The following Saturday after Del and DeeDee saw Jumper, a huge truck pulled up at the Orlis farm and stopped. DeeDee, who was in the living room, saw it first.

"Danny!" she squealed in delight. "Danny! Kay! There's a truck here!"

"Who're you trying to kid?" Doug called from the kitchen.

"I'm not trying to kid anyone. If you don't believe it, come out here and see for yourself." She started down the steps, the others right behind her.

The truck driver climbed out of the cab. "Are you Danny Orlis?"

"That's right."

"I've got three saddle horses for the Davis triplets," he continued, "in care of Danny Orlis."

"See!" DeeDee exclaimed. "What did I tell you? Our horses are here!"

She and the boys crowded close to the big truck, eyes round and voices high pitched.

"This is great, isn't it?" Del said to no one in particular.

Before anyone could answer, the truck driver continued. "Now, if you'll tell me where to unload these horses, we'll get 'em out of my truck so I can be on my way. I've got a lot of driving to do before night."

Danny had him back the truck up to a loading chute near the barn and helped him take the horses down the ramp. The saddle ponies were well trained and unloading them was only the work of a moment or two. The triplets had been talking excitedly, but when the first horse emerged from the trailer they fell silent, staring as though they could not quite believe what was happening.

The driver handed DeeDee the halter rope of the first. "If this horse is yours, you'd just as well start taking care of him." He got out his bills and leafed through them.

"Is there something for me to sign?" Danny asked.

He nodded. "I've got some more stuff for you, too. Oh, yes, here it is. I've got some saddles and a big box of some kind of gear. Don't know for sure what's in it."

DeeDee's eyes widened. "Oh, Danny! Isn't this wonderful?"

"It certainly is."

"It's the most wonderful thing that ever happened to us," she repeated. "I'm still afraid that I'm going to wake up and find that it isn't true."

Danny Orlis put his arm about DeeDee's slim shoulders and squeezed her affectionately. It wasn't that he loved her any more than the boys. He was sure of that. But there was a father-like bond between him and DeeDee that wasn't there as far as Doug and Del were concerned. He couldn't quite understand it. Somehow, they seemed to have an understanding between the two of them. Danny knew that DeeDee didn't think any more of him than she did Kay, but she seemed to have a need for him that was a little different than her need for Kay. Danny felt it unmistakably, and he was sure that DeeDee did, too. But he still didn't understand it.

While the boys helped unload the box of saddles, Danny signed the freight bills, and the truck driver was on his way once more. Only then did the missionary pilot speak again. "Want some help getting those saddles out of the boxes?" he asked.

"Thanks," Del said, grinning, "but I think we can manage."

Doug borrowed Del's pocketknife and ripped the top out of the cardboard carton with it. "What do you know! Uncle Clarence didn't send us the old saddles we used at the ranch. These are brand new!"

All three of them were laughing and talking at the same time.

"I was glad enough to get the horse," Del said, "I sure didn't expect a saddle, too. I figured we'd be riding bareback until we earned enough money to buy some saddles."

Danny got a claw hammer and began to knock the top boards off the crate that held the rest of the gear. There were bridles, extra halters, saddle blankets and several hard-twist lariats. While Danny worked, the boys crouched beside him. DeeDee was little interested in the box of gear. She stood at the corral fence, watching the horses.

"It was sure nice of your Uncle Clarence to send these horses up to you," Danny said. "I always wanted a saddle horse but didn't have one."

"You can ride one of ours, if you want to," DeeDee told him.

"That's one offer Kay and I just might take you up on."

* * *

The next several days the kids rode their ponies every chance they had. Del, however, still took an hour or so every evening to go out and look for Jumper. He found the places where the deer usually fed, and at night after supper he would go out there alone, standing in the brush out of sight until the deer came into the clearing to graze.

Jumper was among them. Even from some distance away Del spotted him almost instantly. There was something different about the way his once-tame deer stood and the way he held his head that set him apart from the others.

The first two or three nights, Del remained as motionless as possible. He let Jumper see him but made no move that might frighten the timid creature. Once it seemed that Jumper was beginning to get accustomed to his presence, he began to move closer, a cautious step or two at a time. Every movement he made was slow and deliberate – natural movements that would let the deer know he wasn't going to bring any harm to him.

As time passed, Jumper calmed. Other deer had long since quit coming to that particular place to feed, but Jumper still returned at about the same time every day. He grew less and less nervous about Del being in the area. In fact, the half-grown deer began to look for Del as soon as he came out of the brush. His actions were much the same as those of a person looking for a familiar landmark or a friend.

Del was very much aware of the gradual change in Jumper's attitude toward him and of a softening of his suspicion. Yet, he was as careful as ever. Perhaps even more so.

At last, the boy was able to move close enough

so Jumper could hear him. When that happened, he began to talk to the deer soothingly. Jumper couldn't understand the words, he knew, but he would finally recognize the friendliness of Del's voice.

"How are you, Jumper, old boy?" he would say softly. "That's it, fella. Go ahead and eat. It's not going to be long until there'll be snow on the ground. Then it won't be so easy for you to fill that fat little stomach of yours."

The task of reassuring the timid half-grown deer was a slow one that took days, and Del soon had lost track of how many hours he had spent out in the woods in the painstaking attempt to convince Jumper that he wasn't going to hurt him. The progress was so slow that Del couldn't mark it from one afternoon to the next. At times it seemed that he was never going to be able to get Jumper to approach him again.

But after a time, he realized that he finally was able to get much closer to the little deer without frightening him. At last, he was so close he could almost reach out and touch Jumper. Yet, he still did not hold out his hand or make any effort to touch him. Del didn't want to undo the progress he had made by becoming impatient.

From time-to-time Danny and Kay and his brother and sister questioned him curiously about Jumper.

"We're doing all right, I guess," he said. "He doesn't run from me anymore when I get close to him."

"Then you've probably got him tame now," DeeDee

said. "Why don't you put a halter or a rope on him and finish taming him that way?"

"That's what I was thinking," Doug put in. "How about it? Would you like to have me go out and help you catch him? If we rope him and bring him back to the barn, we won't have any trouble taming him. We could work with him every afternoon. It wouldn't be long until he'd be following us around like one of the calves."

Del shook his head quickly. "I should say not. If we try to force him that way, it would ruin everything."

"But it's taking so long," his brother protested. "It doesn't seem to me as though you're getting any place. It would drive me nuts to fool around like that."

Del smiled. "I'm not in any hurry. I've got plenty of time."

Danny nodded his approval. "It might take a little longer your way, Del, but I know it's the key to working with any wild creature. He's naturally suspicious of you. You've got to prove to him that he doesn't have to be, and it's going to take time. If you try to force things, you'll only cause trouble. You've got to gain his confidence before you get anywhere with him."

* * *

By this time the football team had moved into their regular season. After a shaky start, Doug began to do very well. He caught a couple of passes and was able to score the winning touchdown on a long run in the first game. In the same game Joe Peters, the running back, hurt his leg. It wasn't a particularly serious injury, but it was enough to take him out of play for several weeks.

After the game the coach asked Doug to wait in the locker room until the others were gone.

"I'd like to talk to you alone," he said quietly.

Doug eyed him but did not reply. This was something that had never happened before and it bothered Doug more than he even realized himself. As he showered and dressed, it was all he could think about.

At last, the other fellows were gone, and he and the coach were alone together.

"You–you wanted to talk to me?" Doug asked, uneasily.

The coach nodded. "I like the way you play football, Doug. You give the game everything you've got."

"I try to play as hard as I can all the time," the boy admitted. "I don't think I do as well as I did in basketball, but it's not because I don't try."

"That's the thing that has attracted my attention. You're in there all the time. I like that." The football coach paused. "Tell me, have you ever thought of trying out for the backfield?"

Doug shook his head.

"I haven't thought about any position especially," he answered. "When I came out for the team you said you thought I should play end, so that's where

I played. But it doesn't make any difference to me – just as long as I get to play."

"I remember now that I was the one who put you at end. Now, I wonder if you'd like to take a try at running back?"

Doug was not sure he had heard correctly. "You– you mean you want *me* in the backfield?"

"That's right – if you'll do it."

"Oh, you won't have to worry about that. I'll do it if I can. It doesn't make any difference to me where I play, as long as I get a chance to play."

"Good. We'll see how it goes in practice tomorrow afternoon."

Del, who had been waiting outside for his brother, was curious about the delay.

"The coach wanted to talk to me."

"What did you do this time?"

"It wasn't anything like that. He just wanted to know if I'd play in the backfield until Joe's able to get back in the lineup."

"Oh." Del spoke woodenly. His cheeks colored and, for an instant, jealousy welled within him. He didn't see why Doug had to have all the athletic ability and he didn't have any. He didn't see why he had to be such a lousy player it wouldn't do him any good to go out. He wouldn't make the team.

That night as they walked home together, Del was very quiet. He shouldn't feel the way he did about Doug, he knew, but he did. Having a brother get ahead of him in everything was almost more than a fellow could bear. He savagely kicked a stone down the graveled road.

CHAPTER 5

UNEXPECTED WITNESS

The entire town of Fairview could talk about little else than the Johnny Larson trial. Fritz McCloud had been so well liked in the community that feeling was still running very high. Everywhere Danny and Kay went, people were talking about it. Most of them were agreed that Johnny should be dealt with severely as an example to the rest of the high school fellows in Fairview.

This bothered Kay a great deal. "I feel so sorry for the Larson family that I can hardly stand it."

Danny walked to the living room window and looked out. "That's the way it is with sin," he began, more to himself than to his wife. "It has its way of leaving its mark. It affects innocent people as much or more than those who are actually guilty. I'm thinking of the loved ones of the person who has sinned.

And in this case the loved ones of Fritz McCloud. It's a bad deal all the way around."

For a time Kay continued to polish the silver. "I've been thinking about Connie McCloud, too. Do you think she'll come back for the trial?"

Danny shook his head. "I don't think so. Actually, there isn't any reason for her to come."

At that moment DeeDee thrust her head in the door. "Danny, have you seen Del and Doug?"

"Not since I got home."

Anger flecked her black eyes. "They were going for a ride with me this evening."

Kay looked up. "Oh, they saddled their horses and rode down by the lake half an hour or so ago."

DeeDee's young face clouded. "Just wait until I get to talk to them! Just wait! They promised that they'd take me along!" With that she was gone, storming across the yard in the direction of the barn.

Danny Orlis watched her affectionately. "You know, it was a great day when God made it possible for us to take the triplets in to live with us."

Kay smiled. "I still thank Him every night for them."

"And to think, He gave us a place like this where we can raise them," Danny added. "It's almost too good to be true."

* * *

The Larson trial was scheduled for Friday afternoon. That morning, however, there was some talk that it might have to be postponed. Jerry Berquist, the son of the local county attorney, had taken sick during football practice the night before and had been taken to the hospital in an ambulance.

Stories about him spread quickly over Fairview. Some said the illness was serious. Others said that it was only exhaustion, and that Jerry would be back in school Monday morning. Some had it that he was to be taken to Minneapolis by ambulance or plane and that the trial would have to be postponed once more.

There was some truth behind all the gossip. Jerry was very ill, there was no doubt of that. The doctor had spent most of Thursday night at the hospital with him. While no decision had been reached regarding the advisability of getting him to a specialist, there was serious talk of flying him to Minneapolis.

Mr. Berquist contacted Danny about noon. "I was just talking to the doctor. He tells me that we might have to fly Jerry to Minneapolis on short notice. He's going to check him again at one o'clock. If he isn't better, he'll have to be flown to the Twin Cities, and there isn't another pilot in town at the moment, Danny." The attorney paused. "Do you suppose you could take him for us?"

"I'll have to get permission from my superiors," Danny Orlis said, "but I'm sure they'll give it for an emergency."

Mr. Berquist seemed visibly relieved. "Good. I don't know whether it will be necessary or not, but it's reassuring to know that the plane is available in case we need it."

Danny contacted the mission director and got permission to fly the attorney's son to Minneapolis if he was called upon to do so.

Shortly after lunch Mr. Berquist phoned to say that the doctor had called in two other doctors for consultation. It was decided that Jerry's condition did not warrant the trip – at least at the moment.

Practically everyone in town thought Mr. Berquist would ask for a continuance of the trial, but he did not. He appeared in court at the appointed time, concern tightening the lines about his eyes.

Danny and Kay both went to the trial. They had heard all the rumors floating about how Johnny was going to try to get out of paying the penalty for what he had done. The most prevalent story was that he was going to plead innocent. It said that his parents had hired one of the shrewdest attorneys in the area, a man who had a reputation for getting verdicts of innocent for his clients.

Johnny, however, surprised everyone by pleading guilty to the charge. Lester McCloud surprised those present even more by appearing as a character witness for the young man who had been driving the car that killed his son.

Mr. Berquist stared at him incredulously. "Do

you mean to tell me that you are here as a witness in behalf of the boy who actually killed your son?"

"Yes, sir." Mr. McCloud's voice was loud and clear.

"Don't you realize that if Johnny hadn't been drunk that night your son would still be alive?" the county attorney asked.

"I'm very much aware of that," Lester answered. "But there are some other things I know about Johnny Larson that give me an entirely different picture of him. I know that he accepted Christ as his personal Savior. He has been in our home many times since-since Fritz' death. I have had an opportunity to get well acquainted with him."

A stunned silence settled over the courtroom. The attorney did not question Lester McCloud but waited for him to continue.

"I want you to know that I did not come here at the request of the defendant, his parents or his attorney."

Mr. Berquist eyed him curiously. "Then why are you here?"

"I believe in Johnny Larson and the change that has come into his life. For that reason, I asked to be put on the stand to testify in his behalf."

Surprise rippled across the crowd. It was half a minute before the county attorney could go on.

"Would you mind telling us why?"

"Not at all. I have come here because I'm convinced that Johnny Larson has been completely rehabilitated. Johnny has accepted Christ as his personal Savior, has taken an active part in the work at our church, and has given every evidence of Christian growth."

"Couldn't this be an attempt on Larson's part to impress people – and you, in particular – that his life is different? Couldn't this be a means of trying to get this court to be lenient with him?" suggested the attorney.

Mr. McCloud shook his head. "Johnny made no effort to get me to come here and testify for him. As far as he knew, I would have been testifying against him. He didn't even ask about that. And he didn't plead innocent. As far as I am concerned, Johnny Larson has proved himself."

The judge heard the balance of the evidence and announced that he was ready to give his decision. The people in the courtroom waited breathlessly while he called Johnny to the bench.

"I find the defendant, John Larson, guilty as charged," he announced clearly.

Emotion rippled across the crowd. Mrs. Larson gasped audibly.

It was a moment before the judge continued, "Sentencing will be postponed for two weeks pending an examination of John Larson by the area parole officer."

Court was dismissed and the crowd filed outside. People were talking in low tones. Almost everyone in the courtroom had expected the verdict, but they had been looking for Johnny to be sentenced that afternoon. This was something unusual.

"You don't suppose that judge'll let him off, do you?" a man behind the Orlises asked his companion.

"Search me. I can't figure out what got into Lester McCloud. He must've been out of his mind, doing what he did today."

"You can say that again. I figured he thought more of his kid than that. But you can never tell what these religious fanatics are going to do."

Danny turned quickly to stare at them. It was all he could do to keep from breaking into their conversation and try to explain what prompted Lester to do as he did. But he said nothing. They wouldn't have understood, anyway, he told himself. There were things those who weren't Christians simply could not understand. This was one of them.

Once they were outside and away from the crowd Kay spoke. "Did you expect that to happen, Danny?"

"I didn't know for sure what was going to happen," he replied. "As a matter of fact, I didn't have any idea of what the judge would do."

They got into the car to start home.

"What do you think this means?" Kay wondered aloud.

"I don't know for sure, but I think it was probably the best that anyone could have expected for Johnny's sake. He had pleaded guilty. The judge had to find him guilty. He didn't have any choice in the matter. But the fact that the judge has asked for an investigation before sentencing shows that he is weighing Lester's testimony heavily. I think it means there is a good possibility that the sentence might be quite light."

Danny and Kay were just pulling away from the curb when Pastor Reeves drove up and stopped to ask about the Berquist boy. He had heard that Danny was to fly him to Minneapolis.

"They haven't come to a definite decision yet, as far as I know," Danny informed him.

"I see." The pastor started to drive away but paused. "I've got to go out of town for a day or two, but the next time you see Mr. Berquist tell him that I'm praying for Jerry, will you?"

"I'll do that."

* * *

In the hospital room Jerry Berquist lay very still and quiet on the narrow white bed. The technician had just been in his room drawing more blood samples for another series of tests. A classmate by the name of Mary Owens came in to straighten his room.

Jerry opened his eyes and glanced about. When he saw Mary, he smiled weakly. "Hi."

She looked up. "Hello." She continued her work.

"How'd Johnny's trial come out today?"

She stopped what she was doing and went over to the side of the boy's bed. "I heard a couple of people talking about it a little while ago. I guess he pleaded guilty, but the judge decided to wait a couple of weeks for some kind of an examination or investigation or something before he decides how long Johnny has to go to jail."

It was a moment or two before the boy spoke again. "It sure is tough on old Johnny. You know, Mary, I was supposed to have been with him that night. We were goin' to have a regular beer bust, but I had to work later than usual, so he ran off and left me."

She went back to work without answering him.

"I didn't know how lucky I was until I–I heard what had happened." He breathed deeply. "If I'd gotten off when I thought I was going to, I'd have been right in the soup with Johnny!"

Mary Owens did not reply. She continued to work in silence. The public address system gave a call for one of the doctors and for a time after that all was silent. Mary finished straightening the room but went over to the bed before leaving. She didn't know why she did, except that she and Jerry were in the same class at school.

"How do you feel now, Jerry?" she asked, her voice a thin whisper.

A strange, haunted look gleamed in the boy's eyes. He started to speak but checked himself. It was almost a minute before he could continue. "I was going to lie to you and tell you I feel swell, but you'd know I wasn't tellin' the truth. I feel awful!"

"I'm sorry," she said.

"I'm scared," he continued, his voice a hoarse whisper. "I'm really scared, Mary."

She began to tremble and had to struggle to control herself. He was sick – she could tell by looking at him. He was terribly sick. "I'm praying for you, Jerry," she got up the courage to tell him. "All the Christian kids at school are praying for you."

On other occasions he would have scoffed at her. More than once he had made fun of Mary and the Christians out at school. But now he smiled gratefully. "I used to talk a lot with Fritz McCloud about stuff like that. He was always talking to me about the Bible and going to church and that sort of junk, but it didn't make sense to me." He swallowed hard. "But I can tell you this much. I'd sure feel a lot better now if I had what Fritz had."

Mary's gaze met his, quickly. She had gone to Sunday school and church and had made her decision for Christ. But she never had led anyone to Christ before. She didn't know what to say. And besides, she was still on duty. If the supervisor came in and caught her visiting with a patient, she might even lose her job. "I'll be back in a little while," she told him.

With that Mary left the room and hurried down to the nursing station, where she dialed the pastor's number. Only then did she remember that Pastor Reeves and his wife were out of town and would be gone for several days. With trembling fingers, she found Danny Orlis' number in the book and called him. Hurriedly she told Kay what she wanted.

"I'll have Danny come to the hospital just as soon as he gets in," Kay answered.

"Please tell him to hurry!"

Prayerfully Mary went back to work.

CHAPTER 6

THREE FOR THE LORD

Over at Cedarton Bible Institute Jim heard the outcome of the Johnny Larson trial on the radio just before dinner that evening. He supposed that Connie had heard it, too; but, in case she hadn't, he waited in the hall until she arrived to eat.

She hadn't heard the newscast and was glad to know how the trial had turned out. "What do you suppose they'll do with him, Jim? Will they send him to the reformatory?"

The Morgan boy shook his head. "I don't know about that. I suppose the judge hasn't made up his mind, or he would have pronounced sentence right away."

"Daddy and Mother will feel terrible about that, if he does send Johnny away."

"The judge must have been impressed with your dad's testimony," Jim continued. "The announcer said that he quoted your dad in making his decision to have the probation officer make an investigation into Johnny's life and the family situation at home."

The muscles about Connie's mouth relaxed slightly. "I feel much better about it now. Even if he is sentenced to the reformatory, it won't hurt like it would have a couple of months ago."

"I don't believe I follow you."

"I don't suppose you do. I'm so confused and upset that I don't know whether I make sense to myself or not." She paused and started again. "Dad did everything he could do to help Johnny. If the judge still puts him in the reformatory, we'll have to accept the fact that it's God's will."

"I feel the same way about it as you do."

They went into the dining room and ate together. As they sat across from each other talking about the trial, it was hard for Jim to realize that things weren't the way they had always been between him and Connie. It was so good to be with her again, enjoying her company.

* * *

That night, as soon as Danny got back to the farmhouse, Kay told him about the phone call. Although he had been working hard and was very tired, he drove back to town to the hospital. Mary had slipped back to Jerry's room and told him Danny was coming, so he was waiting for him.

"How're you feeling, Jerry?" the missionary pilot began.

The boy shook his head. "Pretty rough."

Danny pulled up a chair and sat down. "Mary Owens called and told me that you had some things you'd like to talk to me about."

There was a brief silence.

"I was just talking to her." He shrugged indifferently. "I don't guess it was so important."

Danny's gaze met his. "From what I understand, it's very important. You know you are pretty sick, don't you?"

"I–I guess so." There was fear in his young voice. The moment he acknowledged that he was very ill, his tongue seemed to loosen. "I used to talk with Fritz McCloud a lot about being a Christion and–and stuff like that. But I never would let him get through to me. I wanted to run my own life without any inter ference from anybody."

"I know what that's like," Danny acknowledged. "I used to feel the same way."

That admission seemed to form a tenuous bond between Jerry and Danny.

"You did? I didn't think anybody else ever was like that."

"I think you'll find that most people are – only some are stronger willed than others."

"Well, that's the way I was. I wanted to run my own life. And now, when things aren't going too good for me, I–I'm beginning to wish I'd listened to him. You know, Danny, he really had something."

Danny Orlis nodded. "That's exactly right. Fritz did have something. And what he had was the Lord Jesus Christ."

A strange light gleamed in Jerry's eyes.

The missionary began at the very beginning with sin entering into the world and went over the plan of salvation step by step. He showed Jerry how the Bible says that man was a sinner and through sin earned death. He showed him that everyone is a sinner and needs to be saved and that only by putting his trust in the Lord Jesus Christ can he be sure that he will go to heaven.

When Danny finished, the boy's pain-twisted face lighted briefly. "That's what I want, Danny," he murmured. "I want what Fritz had."

To be sure the boy understood exactly what he was doing, Danny went over the plan of salvation yet again, quoting still other verses of Scripture to prove everything he had said.

At last, he looked up, his gaze meeting Jerry's.

"How about it? Is that still what you want? Do you still want to be a Christian?"

The boy smiled weakly. "That's what I want."

Danny stood beside the bed, and together he and Jerry prayed.

* * *

The following morning Danny was just getting dressed when the phone rang and he was called to the airport.

"This is Berquist!" The county attorney was so distraught Danny scarcely recognized his voice. "I just had a call from the hospital. The doctor feels we ought to get Jerry to Minneapolis as quickly as possible."

Danny caught the tone of despair in the man's voice and quickly assured him, "I'll go out and get the plane serviced and warmed up. Have the ambulance bring Jerry out immediately. I'll be ready by the time they get there."

Danny drove to the airport and started the engine. Fortunately, the plane was filled with gas. It wasn't long until the ambulance sped into the drive and up to the plane. Carefully the ambulance attendants put the boy into the mission's Cessna 180.

The doctor called Danny to one side. "I've phoned Minneapolis for an ambulance. It will be waiting for you at the airport when you get there."

The pilot nodded.

The doctor hadn't planned on making the trip to Minneapolis; but, when Mr. Berquist asked him to, he agreed.

Danny Orlis spoke up. "We've only a four-passenger

aircraft. That will mean that either you or your wife will have to stay home."

"It isn't absolutely necessary that I be along," the attorney said, "and there might be something the doctor can do for Jerry."

They got in the plane and Danny took off. He had been flying fifteen or twenty minutes when there was a stir in the back of the plane.

Mrs. Berquist turned quickly. "What's the matter?" she demanded, shouting over the sound of the engine.

The doctor's face was ashen. "We had just as well go back to Fairview," he said slowly. "Jerry is no longer with us."

Mrs. Berquist gasped. "What do you mean?"

He pulled the sheet over Jerry's head.

"He is dead."

* * *

Danny wanted to talk to Mr. and Mrs. Berquist before the funeral; however, he couldn't quite decide whether he should or not. He talked with Kay about it.

"I'd like to tell them what happened with Jerry and ask them whether they have made a commitment of their lives to Christ or not," he said, "but I can't decide whether this is the time. I surely wouldn't want to do anything that would add to their grief. They already have a great enough burden, without my making it any greater."

His young wife came over to him and stood beside him, looping her arm about his waist. "Danny, if there was one thing Jerry could have that he would want more than anything else in the world, now that he's in heaven, what would it be?"

The missionary pilot pulled in a long breath. "When you put it that way, there's only one choice for me."

Danny drove to the county attorney's home prayerfully. He had to admit, even as he walked up the front steps, that he was half hoping they would not be home. But they were. Mr. Berquist came to the door in response to his knock.

There was a cordiality in the county attorney's tone that had never been present before. "Danny, I'm glad you came. I've been wanting to talk to you."

He led the missionary pilot past the relatives who had gathered in the living room. The two men went into the attorney's den and closed the door.

"I didn't get a chance to thank you for taking Jerry to–I mean for–" His voice trailed away.

"That's quite all right."

Mr. Berquist sat down across from Danny. "I've been wanting to tell you to send me a bill for your services and I'll send you a check."

"There's no charge," Danny told him, smiling.

"No charge?" Mr. Berquist could not understand him. "I expected to pay you for taking him to Minneapolis. You can't fly for nothing."

"The mission can't charge you or anyone else,"

Danny explained. "We aren't licensed for that purpose. And we don't make a practice of flying others, except in the case of an emergency. We wouldn't charge, even if we could."

Mr. Berquist opened his notebook and jotted down something. "I've never sent a gift to an outfit like yours in my life, but I'm going to this time. And it'll be for a great deal more than what a commercial air taxi would have charged – I can tell you that."

"It would be appreciated, I'm sure," Danny told him, "but there's no need for it."

There was another long silence.

"I guess you realize that this is one of the most difficult times in our lives, Orlis."

"I'm sure it is."

The other man's expression changed. "There's something that's been bothering me ever since this happened. My wife and I talked about it last night for a long while." He flexed his big fists impulsively. "How could Lester McCloud come into court and plead for mercy for the boy who was responsible for his son's death?"

"I'm sure he's made of the same stuff you or I are, Mr. Berquist."

Danny would have continued, but the other man broke in. "If I'd have been in his place I wouldn't have slept until I had that Larson kid behind bars for as long as I could have gotten the judge to send him."

"Lester McCloud is a Christian," Danny said, simply.

A strange look gleamed in the county attorney's eyes. "I've always considered myself a Christian, too; but, if that's the sort of thing being a Christian means, I don't know whether I'd qualify or not."

Danny took a pencil from his pocket and fingered it. There was a prayer on his heart as he spoke. "I've got a little story I would like to tell you about Jerry," he began.

Mr. Berquist got quickly to his feet. "Just a minute. Let me get my wife before you tell it."

When the two of them returned to the den a moment or so later, Danny told them about Mary Owens and how she got to talking with Jerry when she was cleaning in his room the day before he died. "Jerry knew how sick he was and told her that he was desperately frightened."

Mrs. Berquist caught her breath sharply. "I thought he was much more aware of his condition than he would let us know."

"He said that Fritz McCloud had talked with him about the Lord Jesus Christ many times, but that he hadn't listened. He told Mary that he wished he had the same faith Fritz had."

The boy's mother began to cry and her husband stiffened angrily. "Why did you call on us to tell us that?" he demanded. "Don't you think it's hard enough for us as it is?"

"Let me finish. Mary called me after she talked with Jerry that night. I went to the hospital to talk to him."

Mr. Berquist leaned forward; his gaze fastened intently on Danny's.

"I led Jerry to Christ before I left," Danny continued. "He wasn't afraid anymore."

Mrs. Berquist stopped crying. Her husband breathed deeply, but the tortured look did not entirely leave his eyes.

Danny continued as gently as possible. "I debated a long while about coming over here tonight to talk with you. I didn't know whether I should or not. But when I talked it over with Kay, she said she was sure Jerry would have wanted me to." With that he went on to explain the way of salvation.

The boy's parents both listened intently until he finished. Danny was not sure how they were taking what he had said until the county attorney's lips parted and he began to speak, slowly and with measured sentences.

"Is that what Lester McCloud has that made it possible for him to get up on the witness stand and ask the court to be lenient with the boy who was responsible for his son's death?"

Danny nodded. "That's right. Having Christ in the heart makes a man different. Lester and I are close friends, and I happen to know that his natural reaction was the same as yours and that of everyone else in town. But, because he had turned his heart and his life over to Christ, his attitude was different."

Mr. Berquist considered the matter thoughtfully. "I–I've always thought I was a Christian," he said, "because I wasn't a drunk or a wife-beater and hadn't robbed any banks. But there's no use in my kidding you or anyone else, Orlis. I'm not like Lester McCloud."

Danny waited prayerfully. There were times for words and times for silence. This was a time for waiting while the man who sat across from him considered all that he had told him.

The county attorney clenched his fists until his knuckles whitened. "I thought I noted a change in Jerry when we took him to the airport. He was so relaxed and–and so peaceful. I thought it was because he was going to a specialist. Now I see that it was something else."

Mrs. Berquist spoke quietly. "I thought I saw a change in him on the way to the airport, too. At first, I thought it was because his condition was improved."

Danny shook his head. "It was because he had made his peace with God."

They had more questions, and Danny had to turn to his Bible again and again to answer them. Before he left their home that night, both Mr. and Mrs. Berquist knelt and gave their hearts to the Lord Jesus Christ.

CHAPTER 7

JOHNNY RECEIVES HIS SENTENCE

Del continued to work with Jumper. After a time, the half-grown buck became so bold he would allow the boy to walk up to him and put his hand on his head. Del was quite sure that he had waited longer than necessary before touching the timid animal, but he didn't want to lose the progress he had made. He didn't touch Jumper until he had approached him within an arm's length a dozen times or more. Even then, the first time he touched the deer Jumper's eyes rolled in terror and the muscles in his shoulders began to ripple nervously.

Del sensed that the deer was about to turn and flee. He withdrew his hand deliberately and took half a step backward. "Now, Jumper, just simmer down, old boy, simmer down. You're not going to be hurt–"

He continued to talk to him soothingly until

the deer began to relax once more. Then, with great caution, he reached out and scratched Jumper's head with his fingers. Again, the buck tensed, but this time his fear was not quite so apparent. He did not act as though he was about to whirl and dash away.

Gradually, as he saw that Del was not going to make any attempt to restrain him, the muscles in his powerful young shoulders began to relax once more. His eyes returned to normal, and he stuck out his nose inquisitively.

Del relaxed, too. Already he knew that the second major victory had been won. Jumper would never again turn and flee from him.

"Yeah, that's better," he said softly. "You and I are going to be great friends." He fished a piece of candy from his pocket and held it out. Jumper ate it greedily.

Del thanked God that night that He had helped him to win back Jumper's trust. He felt better about it than he had ever believed possible. It was great just knowing that he had tamed his pet deer once more. He felt like telling everyone he met about it, but he knew that wouldn't be wise. There were some fellows who would take advantage of Jumper's lack of fear to shoot him if they got the chance. He didn't want to make the risk of that any greater than it was already.

The next time Del went out to the field where the animal was feeding, the deer looked up quickly. Satisfied that it was Del, he came running toward him. A dozen or so feet away he stopped hesitantly still slightly afraid. His ears twitched and there was uncertainty in his manner. Yet, he remembered the kind treatment and the sweet substance the boy had given him. He looked Del over carefully. Slowly he moved forward, a hesitant step at a time, sniffing inquisitively.

Del grinned at him. "I know what you're after." He fished another piece of candy from his pocket and fed the deer. "You want something to eat, don't you?"

* * *

Doug Davis practiced hard at his new halfback position on the football team. He enjoyed the new role and especially the ball carrying, but it was considerably different than playing at end. He wasn't sure whether he was going to be able to make the grade or not.

But the coach didn't seem to share the doubts that he had. "Next year you'll be our starting back," he assured Doug, "and the following year you ought to be playing on the varsity."

Doug Davis beamed.

* * *

The two weeks the judge had set aside for the parole officer to investigate Johnny's background passed quickly. Danny would have forgotten about the trial had it not been that Lester called him that morning and asked him to go with him.

"I don't want Vivian to go," his friend said. "It's hard enough on her as it is. And to be truthful with you, Danny, I hate to go alone."

"I know just what you mean. I'll be glad to go with you, Lester."

They went to the courthouse about ten-thirty that morning and sat in the courtroom until the judge convened the court. Johnny was there with his parents and attorney. Mr. Berquist and the probation officer were also present.

"We have made an investigation of this young man." The judge spoke solemnly. "Our probation office has found that the boy comes from a good home and has indeed made encouraging strides toward rehabilitation." He paused, peering owlishly over his glasses at Johnny. "We are also taking into consideration the request of Lester McCloud, the father of the late Fritz McCloud." He looked down at Johnny. "Would you please approach the bench?"

When Johnny stood before him, he continued solemnly. "I hereby sentence you to three years in the State Penal Complex."

A gasp went up from Johnny's mother.

"However, I am going to suspend sentence and place you on probation for a similar period. You will be expected to make regular reports to your probation officer and to conduct yourself in such a way that you will prove yourself worthy of the trust we are placing in you."

Danny glanced at his companion. Tears stood in Lester's eyes. He wiped them away with his handkerchief.

Johnny was crying when he came over and shook hands with Mr. McCloud. He tried to thank him, but the words would not come. He stood there helplessly, tears streaming down his cheeks.

Mr. McCloud knew what Johnny was trying to say. "If you really want to thank me, Johnny, live a fine Christian life, the sort of a life Fritz would have lived. That will be all the thanks we ever want from you."

The boy's gaze was steady. "I can't do it alone, Mr. McCloud, but with God's help and your prayers I–I'm going to live the sort of life that will make you proud of me."

* * *

The outcome of Johnny's trial was broadcast on the radio that evening. Jim Morgan and his roommate heard it shortly after they came up from the dining hall to their room.

"Is that the kid who was driving the car that killed Connie's brother?" Quinn asked.

Jim nodded. Connie probably was listening to the radio, too. He wondered how she was taking it. She said she wanted him to be set free, but now that he had been placed on probation Jim couldn't help wondering how she felt about it.

"He got off easy, didn't he?"

Jim nodded again. "A lot easier than I thought he was going to. I figured he'd be put in jail for a year or two, anyway." He got his jacket.

"Going somewhere?"

"I think I'll go over to see Connie for a few minutes."

He asked the receptionist to ring for her and went over to sit down, thinking the evening would be a repetition of what had happened the night of the first trial. However, in a few minutes Connie came to the lounge, her eyes bright and smiling.

"Hello, Jim." Her voice was warm and friendly. "I've been expecting you."

His gaze searched her pretty young face. "You have? How come?"

"I just heard the news."

"You don't act very upset about it."

"I'm not," she replied. "Actually, I'm very much relieved. I would have felt terrible if Johnny had had to spend time in the reformatory."

They moved over to the far end of the room where they could have a measure of privacy.

"I'm sure there are a lot of people back in Fairview who have difficulty in understanding the attitude you and your family have toward Johnny," he said.

"I suppose that's true." Her gaze met his. "I didn't feel right toward him for a long while myself, Jim," she went on, "but I can assure you that during that time I was never more miserable in my life. Hate and bitterness are a lot worse on the people who harbor them than on the ones who are hated."

Jim had never quite thought of it that way, but now that he did, he had to admit that it made sense. Thinking back, he knew that during the times he had been angry with people he had been the most miserable. "I think you've got a point."

They talked idly about Johnny for a time, considering the difficulties he would have in trying to live down his reputation around Fairview and how hard it would be for him to maintain a good Christian testimony.

After a time, Jim glanced at his watch. "Have you got your studying done for tomorrow, Connie?" he asked her. There was a certain breathless note in his voice.

"Most of it. Why?"

"I–I thought maybe you'd like to go out for a cup of coffee or some ice cream."

She hesitated. "I'd like to, Jim." Her eyes were wide and luminous, as though tears were not far away. "I'd really like to, but–"

"But what?"

"You know the reason. We've already gone over that a dozen times."

For a moment he did not speak. When he did, disgust edged his voice. "Have you still got the silly idea that you can't go with me because you've got to do the things God had for Fritz to do?"

She laid a hand on his arm, pleading. "Please, Jim, I've wrestled with this thing for weeks and finally have made up my mind that this is God's will for my life. I simply can't do anything else."

He got to his feet. "OK, Connie. I'll see you around."

The walk back to the boys' dorm was the longest he had ever made in his life.

* * *

Johnny scarcely could believe that the judge had given him a suspended sentence in the drunken driving charge against him. His lawyer had been pessimistic about the outcome of the trial from the first, and so were his parents. He had been even more apprehensive of the outcome than the others. He had been sure that he would spend three or four years in the reformatory for what he had done.

It wasn't that he wanted to go there, but in a way, he felt that it would help to ease the weight of guilt that still hung around his neck. After all, Fritz had lost his life for the drinking Johnny had done. A couple of years would be a small price for him to pay for that. Actually, he knew that even though the judge should put him in jail for ten years, or more, he would never be able to pay for what he had done. It was too terrible – too staggering to the imagination.

But, in spite of all of that, the judge had given him a suspended sentence!

At home that night his mother and dad were still marveling at the attitude the McCloud family had taken.

"I've never seen anything like it in my life," Mr. Larson said. "Mr. McCloud actually got on the stand and testified *for* Johnny."

Mrs. Larson choked and wiped her eyes with her handkerchief. "I wouldn't have believed it if I hadn't heard it myself. I don't think I could have done what he did if the situation had been reversed."

The silence hung over them in a breathless hush.

"I still don't understand it," Mr. Larson repeated.

Johnny pulled in a long breath. "I don't understand it for sure, either."

But it was something he pondered over. It must have something to do with the Christian faith of the McCloud family, but he didn't tell his folks that. They wouldn't understand that, either.

CHAPTER 8

WISE COUNSEL

Every fall Cedarton Bible Institute asked a well-known Bible teacher or evangelist to come to the school and hold special meetings for a week. Classes were suspended or sharply curtailed, and everyone was expected to attend the afternoon and evening meetings.

Connie McCloud found them to be a special blessing. Dr. Whitman, the speaker for that fall, had a most practical approach to the Scriptures. He gave them something to take home – something they could put into practice in their daily lives. Connie appreciated this more than anything else. It seemed to be exactly what she needed for that particular time.

The week was almost over when Jim, with whom she still visited occasionally when they chanced to meet in the hall, suggested that she see the visiting speaker.

"Why should I talk with him?" she asked, uneasy by the insistence in her friend's voice.

"I'd like to have you discuss this thing about you having to take over Fritz' Christian service now that he's gone."

She stiffened. "I know what the Lord would have me do," she informed him coldly. "There's no need of talking with Dr. Whitman or anyone else to learn that."

"I'd still like to have you talk with him. I think you owe it to yourself, even if you don't owe it to me."

She glared at him. "Tell me something, Jim. Have you been talking with Dr. Whitman about me?"

Jim shook his head. "Nope," he retorted quickly. "I don't think I've said more than a couple of dozen words to him at one time. I've shaken hands with him and have told him I've gotten some help from his messages. That's all I've said."

Connie was silent for a time.

"Dr. Whitman isn't going to be swayed by anything I or anyone else would tell him," Jim went on. "So it shouldn't make any difference if I had talked with him. And you shouldn't be afraid to talk with him, Connie. If you're right in what you're thinking, he'll tell you so; and you'll be even more sure that you've done the right thing. And if you're wrong, I'd think you'd want to know it."

Her lips tightened. "Well, I–I'll think about it." Then, lest he think she was conceding, she continued hurriedly, "but I'm not promising anything. You understand?"

"Fair enough."

The rest of the day, despite determined effort on Connie's part to put the subject out of mind, she could think of little else. And when she went to the service that night, she thought she had made up her mind not to see Dr. Whitman privately. However, at the end of the evening service, she found herself seeking out the speaker and asking if she could have an appointment with him.

"It–it's about a personal problem," she explained.

"Of course, I can see you." His smile seemed enhanced by the white of his hair. "When would you like to see me?"

"Any time that's convenient for you."

She had supposed he would give her a time the following day, but instead he glanced at his watch. "How about right now? I don't have anything else planned for this evening."

They went to the business office that had been set aside by the president for counseling. The speaker was in no hurry. He leaned back in his chair and was silent momentarily. When he did speak, his voice was quiet and sympathetic. Connie found herself liking him a great deal. He was even more pleasant personally than he was on the platform. Something about his gentle manner inspired confidence.

"Now, just what is troubling you?"

Suddenly she had difficulty in finding words. It seemed so presumptuous to waste the time of a man like this with her problem. Yet, he seemed to be most concerned. Hesitantly she told him about her brother, Fritz, and the change that had come into his life during the Bible camp program the summer before his death. She told him how Fritz was so burdened for his friends that he became a tremendous personal worker while she grew cold and began to dabble in the things of the world.

Her voice choked now and again as she related the story of the automobile accident that took Fritz' life and the way it had shaken the town of Fairview. She went on to explain how she had come back to the Lord and was now determined to serve Him. All of that was in preparation for what she had really come to talk with him about.

"And I feel that God wants me to do Fritz' work in addition to my own," she continued. "I feel that He wants me to reach the people Fritz would have reached for Christ and witness to those he would have witnessed to."

She paused when she got that far in her account, studying the Bible teacher quizzically. She had expected some sort of commendation from him – some word that would indicate he felt she had the right attitude and indeed must be in the will of God. Instead, his face was expressionless.

"And what are you doing for the Lord now,

Connie?" he asked. The question was simple enough, but it drove to the very depths of her heart.

"I–" she stammered.

He waited.

"Well," she went on, lamely, "I have my Christian service assignment."

"So do the other students." He leaned forward, his eyes narrowing. "Are you doing anything else for God?"

Reluctantly she shook her head.

"You've no doubt had a great shock in the loss of your brother," he told her, "and I know that in cases like this it is sometimes difficult for one to get hold of himself." He paused, thinking out carefully what he was going to say. "The thing we need to keep in mind, always, is that God has a plan for the life of each believer. In that plan He has a work we are to do. But He does not expect any of us to do the work He outlined for someone else."

Her eyes widened. "But–"

"In fact, in the case of an individual like your brother, who was living a dedicated Christian life, I am convinced that he had finished his work."

"But he was so young," she protested. "He hadn't even started–"

"That's the way man thinks. Fritz' work was done, Connie, or God wouldn't have taken him home. And, if Fritz' work is done, it is not God who is telling you that you have to pick up Fritz' load and carry it in addition to your own." He smiled, great understanding coming into his face as he did so. "No, my dear, God had a work for Fritz. He expected him to do it and, from what you tell me, he did it to the best of his ability. God doesn't want you to carry Fritz' load. He wants you to carry your own. He has a plan for your life and is going to be looking for you to carry it out."

Connie felt the color rise in her cheeks.

"Thank you." She ended the interview abruptly by getting to her feet. "Thank you very much." With that she walked out of the office hurriedly and closed the door, leaving Dr. Whitman sitting there.

She hadn't realized how angry she was until she was out of the building and halfway across the campus to the girls' dorm. Dr. Whitman might be an outstanding Bible teacher and all of that, but he certainly didn't know much about counseling. After all, she wasn't a child. She was a mature young woman who had prayed the matter through.

It wasn't what *she* wanted. What person in her right mind would *want* to carry such a burden? She felt that it was God's will. She was supposed to give up Jim and any hope of marriage in the future. She was to dedicate her life to doing the work God had for Fritz. Why else would He have laid such a burden on her heart?

Connie's mind was still rolling as she went up to her room and got ready for bed. She knelt to pray, but everything was so confused and bewildering that it was almost impossible for her to talk to God. All she could think about was what Dr. Whitman had said. And he had been so positive! As though there was no possible chance that he was wrong!

As Connie tossed restlessly in bed trying to go to sleep, his arguments churned endlessly through her consciousness. God didn't want her to do Fritz' work. The task he was to do was done – finished – in spite of the fact that some of those he witnessed to had not yet made decisions for Christ. God had His plan and will for her own life. That was what she was responsible for, and only what she was responsible for. It may or it may not include Jim, but that was another matter. It had nothing whatever to do with Fritz.

She knew what she would have to do the next morning. She would have to see the guest speaker and apologize for the rude way she had treated him the night before.

And Jim! Tears filled her eyes as she thought of him. Momentarily, they trembled on the tips of her eyelashes before they started to trickle down her cheeks.

Quietly Connie slipped out of bed and knelt to pray again. This time there was no hesitation – no faltering as she poured out her heart to God. When she went back to bed, she drifted off to sleep almost immediately – for the best rest she had had in months.

The next morning, she got up a few minutes earlier

than usual, dressed and had her devotions alone. She went over to the dining hall before her roommate was ready and stood inside the door in a place where she could see everyone who came in. It seemed as though Jim would never get there.

When he did come, she was scarcely ready to face him. Her breath was coming in short, quick stabs and her forehead was moist from perspiration. For the space of a heartbeat, she felt as though she could not speak.

"Hi, Jim." Her voice was thin and unnatural. "Have you eaten yet?"

He stared briefly at her, surprised by the sudden show of friendship. "Nope," he replied. "I haven't been up that long. How about you?"

"I've been waiting for you," she replied frankly. Questions widened his gaze, but he made no comment at her strange remark. Instead, he took her arm and guided her to a table away from the others. They would be alone only for a few short moments before the rest of the chairs would be taken by noisy fellows and gay, laughing girls. Somehow Jim sensed those few moments to be very important.

Once they had asked the blessing, she looked up at him. "I suppose you're wondering why I waited to talk with you this morning," she began.

"Well," he said, grinning crookedly, "the thought had come to me."

"I–I talked with Dr. Whitman last night," she went

on. There! It was out. Now she had to go on. She saw how curious he was, but she could not blurt out the way she felt or what the speaker had said to her. She had to tell it in her own way to try to explain why she had come to a change of heart.

"He made me awfully mad, Jim," she told him. "I actually got up in the middle of our interview and–and walked out on him."

His lips tightened. "You must not have approved of what he had to say."

Her lips trembled until she found it difficult to go on. "Last night," she said at last, "I lay awake for several hours thinking about what he said. It was just as though his words turned God's searchlight on my life and showed me every hidden little nook and cranny that I'd never seen before. I know now that I've been terribly wrong in trying to do Fritz' work for the Lord."

Jim could scarcely believe he was hearing what she was saying. He stared at her incredulously.

"He made me see that I was trying to make a martyr of myself and that self-pity, not a desire to serve God, was really the motivating force behind what I was doing. He made me see that although I've done a lot of talking about doing Fritz' work, I haven't actually done much of anything for the Lord, except talk about how I was going to serve Him. I've been too busy trying to punish myself for what happened to Fritz and feeling sorry for myself because I thought I couldn't have a normal life like other girls." She would have gone on, but the look on Jim's face stopped her.

"You'll never know how long I've prayed that you would see this thing as it really is."

She laid a hand on his arm, with a tenderness that thrilled him. "Will you forgive me?"

"You know the answer to that!" His heart was singing!

CHAPTER 9

A CHANCE TO MAKE GOOD

During the days that immediately followed the trial, Johnny stayed at home most of the time. He hadn't been to school during the weeks of the trial because of the strong possibility that he would be sent to the reformatory. That and the attitude of many of the parents at having him in school associating with the other kids when he was under indictment for vehicle homicide made it seem best that he stay away.

It was difficult for him to go back to school after the trial, too, in spite of what had happened there.

Johnny was more bored than he had ever been, staying at home, but he could not bring himself to go out, regardless of how hard he tried. He couldn't stand the thought of having to face people on the street.

There were times when he felt like running away. At least he could get away where he wouldn't have to continually meet people who knew him and knew what a terrible thing he had done. However, if he had left the county without permission of the parole officer he'd have been in worse trouble than ever. Staying in Fairview and the surrounding area had been one of the conditions of his parole. And, anyway, he was done with that sort of thing. He wasn't going to break the law anymore if he could help it.

So Johnny stayed at home reading and watching television until he was so nervous and bored he felt he could climb the walls. His mother tried to talk with him, but that didn't help much, even though he tried to keep her and his dad from knowing how he felt. Finally, he decided that he had to talk with some of the guys his own age; some of the fellows he used to run around with, maybe.

Toward the end of the week, he put on his parka and went down to the filling station where his old gang used to hang out. There would be several of them there. He knew that before he got close enough to see their cars. There was always somebody loafing around there. They'd probably be talking about the big party they had gone on last night, or the one they were having over the weekend. That would give him a chance to talk to them about what Christ had done for him. Maybe he'd be able to give his testimony the way Fritz McCloud used to do.

The very thought of helping his old buddies warmed him inwardly. It wouldn't make any difference to him if they laughed at him. He'd make them see they were just kidding themselves when they thought they were getting away with something by drinking.

Three of the fellows were at the station. He knew who they were and that they'd skipped school that morning for something or other. Maybe to sleep off a hangover of the night before or, at least, to make someone else think that was why they were playing hooky.

He quickened his pace.

In the station he spoke to the old gang, his smile flashing warmly. They eyed him but did not return his greeting. There was no doubt that they had heard him. They were standing less than a dozen feet away. They looked him over distastefully, as though there was something unclean about him. He cringed under the unfriendliness of their eyes.

"Hi." He spoke again.

Finally, Dick Barber spoke, grudgingly, as though he had done so because he couldn't avoid it.

"How have things been going?" Johnny asked.

"OK, I guess."

That was all. There was no warmth, no friendliness in his voice. It surprised Johnny to have Dick treat him that way. He had always supposed Dick was a good friend of his. They had gone on many drinking parties together.

But Dick was different than Johnny had ever seen him. He acted reluctant even to talk to the Larson boy. Johnny felt the ice squeeze about his very being.

He wanted to run and hide – to get so far away from Fairview and that particular filling station that he would never see either of them again. But he couldn't leave. He had to stay there and face them.

"Let's get out of here," Tyler said, studying Johnny's eyes scornfully.

Johnny remembered Tyler well. He had been on most of the drinking parties. The last time, a week or so before the fatal accident, Tyler had been so drunk the guys had to carry him into the house when they took him home.

"Come on," Tyler continued, "let's go someplace where the company's better."

With that they went out the door, leaving Johnny and the station attendant alone. The man behind the cash register glared at him but did not speak.

Johnny turned and stumbled out the door. The wind was sharp and wearing an icy edge, but he scarcely noticed it. This was worse than the time in jail after the accident and before he was released on bond. It was worse than the trial. These were his old friends. His old buddies! And now they wouldn't have anything to do with him. He couldn't go back and face them again. He'd die first!

Sunday morning Johnny didn't even want to go to Sunday school and church. He wouldn't have if Lester McCloud hadn't stopped by for him. And he couldn't turn down Mr. McCloud. Not after what he had done for him. It was a strange thing when the father of the boy he had killed became his very best friend. That was something he still didn't understand.

The kids at church spoke to him all right, and some of the congregation seemed to go out of their way to greet him and try to make him feel welcome. He answered them and tried to think of things to say to them, but he felt funny inside. He wasn't sure whether they spoke to him because they wanted to or because they thought they ought to.

The next day he decided to go out and try to find a part-time job – something that would permit him to help his folks by taking care of himself, at least.

His mother knew how hard it was for him and tried to talk him into waiting for a while. "You don't have to be in such a hurry to get work. Why don't you wait until you're a little more comfortable around people?"

He shook his head. "I can't wait, Mom. I've got to do something. I've got to start taking care of myself, for onc thing, and I ought to be paying back some of the money Dad spent on me for the trial and that sort of thing."

"We haven't asked you to do that, Johnny."

"No, you haven't, but that doesn't make it any less my responsibility. I've got to do it. Don't you see?" His voice rose. "Dad has to work hard for his money. I can't sponge off him anymore."

Steeling himself to the hostility he knew he would face, he went out that morning to find work. It was noon when he came back, shuffling along the snow-lined walk, hands thrust deep in his pockets and his head down. Mrs. Larson saw him coming up the walk and her heart ached for him. She knew immediately that it hadn't gone well with him.

He came slowly into the house, kicking the snow from his shoes on the porch. Dejection marred his sensitive young face.

Mrs. Larson's heart ached as she read the anguish in her son's young face. There was no need to ask him whether he had gotten work or not. She could read the answer in the sag of his shoulders and the dullness of his eyes.

"I'm glad you're home, Johnny." She tried to sound cheery and undisturbed. "Lunch is almost ready."

It was as though he had not heard her. He stumbled into the kitchen and stood by the table. For an agonizing instant or two, she was afraid that he had been drinking again. Then she saw that it was only dejection that caused him to act so strangely.

"I've been all over town, Mom," he said, his voice trembling, "but it doesn't make any difference how badly anybody needs help. When they see me, they change their minds."

"I'm sure that must be your imagination, Johnny. The people in Fairview are our friends. They wouldn't treat you that way."

"You just come with me, if you don't believe it!" He sank wearily into a chair near the table. "Nobody in this town will hire me! They wouldn't hire me if I'd work for nothing!"

She came over and sat across from him, striving to keep the concern from her own eyes.

"I don't think it's because of–of what happened that keeps you from getting work. You want to remember that part-time jobs are particularly hard to find. Most places want to hire a person who can be trained as a full-time employee. They want someone who will stay with them permanently. I'm sure that's your problem."

His gaze met hers. He wasn't convinced that she was right, but there was no use in making her feel worse than she did already.

"I've been out of school for three weeks now," he said. "Maybe they won't even let me go back. Did you ever think of that?"

"Oh, no," she retorted quickly. "Dad talked to the members of the school board. They said everyone was looking for you to return. You are as welcome as anyone else."

"They probably told him that just to get him off their necks. When I actually try to go back, they might change their minds." He was breathing heavily. "I don't think there's anyone in this town who wants to have anything to do with me, and I can't say that I blame them."

Mrs. Larson got up and turned off the gas flame under her percolator. "Have you thought about going to see Lester McCloud? He's been so very kind. Maybe he could help you."

* * *

That night Mr. McCloud drove out to the Orlis home and asked to talk to Danny alone.

"Johnny was in to see me this afternoon. He was very discouraged." Lester went on to tell how Johnny's old friends had treated him and the trouble the boy was having in finding work. "Not being able to get a job is the very worst thing that could happen to Johnny right now. He wants to help his dad by taking some of the financial load this trial has cost, but nobody will hire him."

Danny knew that what Lester said was true. Johnny had to have work and feel that he was able to make some sort of contribution, and he needed to have something to do to fill his time after school.

"Do you have any ideas as to how we can help him?" he asked.

Mr. McCloud leaned forward; and, although the study door was closed and the others in the house were in the living room with the radio on, he lowered his voice. "Vivian and I were talking about it this evening at the supper table. If we could help him get a job and get in with Christian friends, we'd be giving him a big boost in the right direction."

Danny took a pencil from his pocket and fingered

it thoughtfully. "I don't know of anyone who needs any help at the moment, but I'll sure do what I can."

During the next few days Danny and Lester contacted a number of Christian businessmen about work for Johnny. Several didn't have any openings at the moment. Only one mentioned what the boy had done and used that as a reason for not hiring him.

"It isn't that I don't like Johnny or anything like that," he explained, "and I understand how hard it is for him; but most of my customers thought Fritz was the finest kid in town. I'm afraid I'll lose business if I take Johnny on."

"Even if I ask you to?"

A strange look glimmered in the other man's eyes. "I can't figure you out, Lester. You know there's a lot of talk around Fairview about the way you and your wife have stood up for this boy."

Lester's face hardened. "He needs help, Joe. It's our Christian responsibility to give it to him."

"I know that." Joe's expression changed slightly. "I understand how it is. I don't feel that way, mind you, but a lot of people are wondering. They think Johnny ought to pay for the terrible thing he did."

"Tell me," Lester McCloud went on, "have you talked with him lately?"

"Nope. I can't say that I have."

"He has paid for what he did and, what's more, he'll keep right on paying for it as long as he lives."

Joe hitched forward in his chair and a scowl

showed through his thin smile. "But after all, Fritz was your son!" He spoke accusingly, as though Lester McCloud had forgotten that fact.

"Fritz would have been the first to want to help Johnny. He had been praying for him for months," Mr. McCloud said.

Joe got to his feet, still irritated by his visitor. "I'm sorry, Lester, but I can't help him. My wife would never let me hear the end of it if I did."

So it was, as Mr. McCloud and Danny went from one businessman to another. There were those who were genuinely concerned but had no work for Johnny. There were others who would not have him around because of what he had done.

At last, however, Mr. McCloud found a man who was willing to take a chance on him. Happily, he went to the Larson home and told Johnny about it.

Tears flooded the boy's eyes. "I don't know how I can ever repay you for all you've done for me."

"You can repay both Ted Lohman and me by living a clear-cut Christian life, Johnny," McCloud told him. "That would more than repay us for anything we've done to help you."

When Mr. McCloud was gone, Johnny went to his bedroom and stood before the mirror for a long while, combing his hair. It scarcely seemed possible that Lester McCloud would take time from his busy schedule to find him a job. Him! After the terrible thing he had done to the McClouds!

A prayer welled in the boy's heart – a prayer of thankfulness. He would show Mr. McCloud and his new employer that they had made no mistake when they decided to help him. He dropped impulsively to his knees and began to pray aloud for strength and guidance.

* * *

Danny and Kay were as pleased as Johnny was when they learned that he finally had found part-time work with a Christian employer.

"I'm so glad Ted was able to use Johnny," Kay said. "I was beginning to think there wasn't anyone in town who would hire him."

Danny kicked off his shoes and reached for the slippers beside him. "Well, you can't really blame them. Johnny doesn't have a whole lot going for him when you start talking about his job qualifications. He hasn't finished school yet and he doesn't have training in any particular field. And his reputation isn't exactly the best. I can understand it." Danny picked up the evening paper. "But he's got a job now, working for someone who will be fair with him and give him a chance to make good. That's the main thing."

Kay nodded. "Now, if he would only get rid of those outlandish clothes and get his hair cut!"

Danny looked up, thoughtfully. "That's all very true, Kay, but we've got to keep remembering that

Johnny doesn't come from a Christian background. I don't suppose the thought has ever occurred to him that his clothes and personal appearance can affect his testimony."

* * *

Doug had been waiting eagerly for the basketball season to start. From the first afternoon the coach called practice for the junior high team, he was out for it, throwing himself into the sport with everything he had.

It would be just about perfect if Del would go out for basketball, too, he reasoned. Actually, sports were the first thing that had separated them. It disturbed Doug a great deal. He tried to talk Del into trying out for the team, at home that evening.

"Me, play basketball?" his brother echoed, derision curling his lips. "Hah!"

"You just got off to a bad start last year, that's all that was wrong. I'll bet you'd do OK if you'd try out for the team now."

"That's not the way I see it. I'd be a good prospect, all right – for the girl's team!"

"I'll help you, Del. We'll practice every evening after supper. You'll get onto it soon."

In spite of himself, Del felt his temper begin to build. "As far as basketball is concerned, I'm just not interested."

"But–"

"I've told you a dozen times, I just can't do it. Don't you understand English?"

But his brother was not going to give up that easily. "If you'd just go out for the team and get to play in a game or two, you'd find out that it's a lot of fun."

Del moved in the direction of their bedroom door. "Lay off, will you?"

Doug stared numbly after him. He still had not moved when Danny came into the room a moment or two later.

"Have you done your chores, Doug?"

"I'll get to them right away."

Danny saw the concern on his young face. "What's the matter?"

"Nothing." In spite of himself he was close to tears. "Nothing at all."

"Maybe I can help." Danny went over to a chair and sat down.

"It's about Del," the boy began. "I've never seen anybody so stubborn."

Danny waited for him to continue.

"He could play basketball, if he'd just go out for the team and put forth a little effort. There's nothing to it."

The pilot smiled. "Maybe Del doesn't want to play basketball. Did you ever think of that?"

Doug acted as though he hadn't heard what the missionary pilot said. "I told him I'd help him. I told him I'd work out with him till he got good enough to make the team, but he's so stubborn he won't listen to me! He won't do a thing I want him to do!"

Danny Orlis took a minute or two before answering. "There's something I'd like to talk to you about, Doug, that might help you. You enjoy basketball, but that doesn't mean that Del does."

"He could if he wanted to."

"God has made each of us differently. Del would much rather be out with his horse or Jumper. He never could be as good in athletics as you are – or at least that's the way it seems to me. And you probably could never have the way with animals that he has."

"But–"

"We have to realize that God has given us different talents and abilities. Our responsibility is to see that we use what God has given us to His honor and glory."

CHAPTER 10

REAL FRIENDS FOR JOHNNY

Del was sitting in the bedroom he shared with his brother, Doug, staring silently at the floor. Doug could talk all he wanted to, but he wasn't going to get him out on the basketball floor again where he'd make a fool of himself. That was all there was to it. He knew that was what Doug wanted to do. He wanted to show everybody how much better he was at playing basketball than Del. Well, he wasn't going to get away with it.

When Del heard his brother's footsteps approaching, he picked up his math book, turned quickly to the next day's assignment and pretended to be studying. Doug came into the room slowly and closed the door.

"Hi."

There was no answer.

Doug walked across the room and sat down. "I'd like to talk to you for a couple of minutes, Del."

Del turned from the desk, eyes blazing. "If you want to talk about basketball, forget it. I don't plan on trying out for the team, so you can be the big star all by yourself."

Doug bristled. "You don't have to get so huffy about it."

"OK. OK. I don't have to get so huffy. Now, will you please lay off so I can study?"

The next morning when Doug got up, he was surprised to see that Del already was dressed and gone. Doug went into the kitchen where Kay and DeeDee were getting breakfast.

"Where's Del?" he wanted to know.

His sister looked up "He said he wanted to check on Jumper."

Doug pulled out a chair and dropped into it. He knew well enough that Del wasn't around because he didn't want to be with him. That was the reason he'd gone out to look at that deer of his.

The basketball-playing Davis boy shrugged. If that was the way Del wanted it, OK. He didn't have to be around him. He'd do a good job of leaving him alone. That's what he'd do!

Del came into the house in time for breakfast, stomping the snow from his boots.

Kay turned to him. "You'd better hurry, Del. The bus will be here before you've finished breakfast."

"I got worried about Jumper." He went to the table and sat down, without looking directly at Doug.

"Worried about him?" Kay said. "Why?"

"When I saw that it had snowed again last night, I got to thinking that he might not be able to get anything to eat, so I went out to see how he was doing."

"If that's what you're worried about, you can stop it now. He'll be able to take care of himself, all right."

The brothers glanced at each other but did not speak.

That afternoon at the close of school, the junior high basketball squad hurried down to the locker room to dress. Doug thought he would be the first one there, but Larry Larson was already there, peeling out of his shirt.

"Hi, Doug." His grin was warm and friendly.

"I don't see how you got here so quick."

Larry laughed. "My brother told me about a shortcut."

They were the first to get into uniform and on the basketball court.

"I didn't remember that you were out for the team last year, Larry."

"I was out, all right." He shot with one hand. The ball arced neatly through the basket. "That was the trouble. I was out after the first cut. But it's going to be different this year. I've been doing a lot of practicing."

Doug took his turn, driving forward to tip the ball in as his first shot missed.

"I sure wish I had somebody to practice with."

"What about Del?"

"Him?" Scorn twisted Doug's face. "As far as he's concerned a basketball is poison."

"Why don't you come over to my house? Johnny'd be glad to help you at the same time he helps me."

"Johnny?" Doug's forehead crinkled.

The life seemed to go out of Larry as the Davis boy mentioned his brother's name. "Yeah, Johnny." He spoke defensively. "Unless you don't want him to help you."

"It's not that at all," Doug said quickly. "I guess I was just surprised to find out that he's your brother."

Larry's lower lip quivered. "I thought everybody in town knew that Johnny's my brother." He paused. "You know, some of the guys can't even come over to my house anymore just because I'm related to Johnny."

That night at home Doug told Danny what Larry had said. "I didn't think people could be so mean," he concluded.

"It isn't the Christian way, Doug. That's for sure." Danny toyed with his cup. "And I'm not excusing the attitude of people like that. When a fellow is down, it's that kind who do their best to keep him down."

"It's not Larry's fault that Johnny got drunk and drove the car that ran into Fritz and killed him."

"That's right," Danny said. "That's exactly right." He paused momentarily. "You know, I can't help thinking about kids who say it's nobody's business what they do. They say it's only their own concern. They're going to live their own lives and if they want to drink and carouse that's their business. But the truth is that none of us can sin without affecting other people." He drew in a deep breath. "Look what Johnny's sin did. It took Fritz McCloud's life and plunged the McCloud family into grief that they probably will never get over. It robbed the church of a consecrated young worker. It brought shame to Johnny and his entire family, taking friends from his younger brother. I could go on and on listing the effect this had on other people."

Doug's young face grew thoughtful. It was some time before he was able to speak. "I'd never thought of it quite that way."

"I'm sure Johnny hadn't either," Danny said, "before Fritz was killed. But you can be sure that he's thought plenty about it since."

DeeDee, who had been listening intently to the conversation, spoke up. "When you think of sin and the effect it has on other people, and especially on those you love, it makes you want to live the way Christ wants you to, doesn't it?"

"It sure does," Danny answered.

* * *

On Saturday morning Danny had to go to the airport to check out the plane for a flight to Canada on Monday. Doug caught a ride to town with him so he could practice basketball with Larry. His new friend was in the basement when Doug got there.

"You *did* come, after all," Larry exclaimed.

"Sure. I told you I would, didn't I?"

Larry began to bounce the basketball subconsciously.

"I figured maybe your folks wouldn't let you come to spend the morning with me when they found out whom you were going to be with. You know, I'm a bad character."

Doug took off his parka. "You don't look bad to me. Besides, Danny and Kay aren't the kind that wouldn't want me to come over here and see you if I wanted to. Danny went out with Lester McCloud to see if he could help find a job for Johnny. That's the kind of a guy he is."

Larry caught the ball and held it. "That Mr. McCloud is some guy. Mom and Dad say they don't know where Johnny would be if it wasn't for Mr. and Mrs. McCloud. They're sure he'd have had to go to the reformatory."

Doug held out his hands and Larry tossed the ball to him.

"You want to remember that Johnny accepted Christ as his Savior. That's the thing that changed Johnny's life and made it possible for them to help him. They wouldn't have been able to do anything for him if it hadn't been for that."

Larry remained motionless for an instant or two.

Then he took a pass from Doug and dribbled to the other side of the basement.

"This is something Johnny showed me how to do last night," he said, changing the subject abruptly. "If a defensive player is crowding you, fake to this side as though you're going to pass him this way. As he starts in that direction, reverse, and come around the opposite side."

Doug and Larry worked together on the maneuver, taking turns until they began to feel that they had mastered it.

* * *

When the basketball game that Tuesday began, Doug took the tip and rifled the ball to Larry, who was moving down the floor at top speed. Larry faked the defensive forward out of the way and passed to Doug who was tied up briefly before getting the pass away. Larry took the ball again and began to dribble deliberately, slowing the fury of the pace.

Doug shook his man long enough to take a throw from the opposite side of the court. Conditions were right to try the new maneuver Johnny had taught to Larry. He faked the defensive man out of position and shot. The ball circled the rim and dropped in to put Fairview ahead by two points.

Neither Larry nor Doug knew that Johnny had

gotten to the game until he shouldered his way onto the floor after the final whistle.

"Hi, Johnny!" Doug's smile was warm and friendly.

Larry broke in. "How'd we do?"

"Not bad." The corners of Johnny's mouth straightened. "Not bad at all. In fact, you both played a pretty good game. You're going to do all right when you get a little more experience."

Doug felt a warm glow come to his being. This was different than hearing a little praise from some guy who didn't know anything about basketball. Johnny had been an outstanding player until he got kicked off the team last season. Everybody said he had been a cinch to be chosen for the all-state quintet. When a fellow like Johnny said they'd done well, there was no doubt about it. They had done OK.

"Hurry and get showered and dressed," he said. "I'll wait for you. I jotted down a few things that I'd like to talk with you about."

While Johnny was waiting, a couple of his old drinking buddies came by. They eyed him stonily but did not speak. The boy's cheeks drained of color and that numbing ache came back in his chest. He wasn't going to let it bother him that they wouldn't speak to him anymore, he told himself doggedly. He was better off without them. He would have been a lot better off if he'd never met them.

Suddenly an uncontrollable urge to turn and leave the building gripped him. He'd go someplace so far away they'd never know where he was. Then they wouldn't be able to hurt him. He turned blindly toward the door.

Johnny would have been gone had the boys not come out at that moment. They were still excited over their victory and the exhilaration of the game. Doug wanted to talk about the way he had played. He asked a dozen questions about the notes Johnny had made, pressing him for specific answers as to what he would have done in each situation.

Johnny answered him quickly and changed the subject to something he felt was far more important. "If you fellows really want to be good basketball players, there's something more important than the way you handle the ball or what you know about the game."

"What's that?" Doug asked.

"Be sure you don't ever start to smoke or drink. Those things'll ruin you quicker than anything I know." He breathed deeply. "All you have to do is to look at me and you'll know that I'm telling you the straight truth."

There was a long silence.

Johnny was thinking about his drinking and the terrible things it had done. It had caused him to get kicked off the basketball team and caused Fritz McCloud to be killed. It had robbed him of any respect or reputation he had in the community. For a time, he wasn't even aware of his companions, so deep was his hurt.

* * *

On Saturday Doug went to spend the morning practicing basketball as usual. Johnny came down to the basement during his noon hour to give them some pointers. When Doug came home that afternoon, Kay was in the living room alone.

She looked up from her sewing and smiled. "I was beginning to wonder if you were going to be home in time for supper."

"I'm not too late, am I?"

She shook her head. "As soon as I finish mending this shirt, I'll start it."

He went over and sat down. "Kay," he said, "don't you think it's about time I had a new pair of jeans."

She looked him over quickly. "Those look all right to me."

He fumbled for words. "Nobody wears this kind anymore. I–I need some white ones."

"White jeans?" Kay echoed. "I don't see why you'd want white jeans. And, to tell you the truth, I can't see anything wrong with the ones you're wearing now."

"They're so-so ordinary. They don't fit right, or anything."

Kay took a deep breath. It was obvious that she wasn't even remotely aware of what he was talking about. "I'll have to talk it over with Danny and see what he has to say."

When Danny came in from the study a short while later, she told him about her conversation with Doug.

"I'm completely confused, Danny," she said. "I don't see anything wrong with the jeans he's got.

And why on earth would he want a pair of white jeans? I'd be doing the laundry every day."

"Don't you know what he's talking about?" Danny asked, laughing. "His old pants don't fit the way he wants them to."

Kay snorted indignantly.

* * *

The following Friday Jim Morgan and Connie McCloud came home from Cedarton Bible Institute for the weekend.

Danny noticed the change in Jim's spirits almost immediately. "It sure is good to see you like your old self, Jim. I don't mind telling you, you were mighty grumpy for a while."

A faint grin toyed with the corners of Jim's mouth. "I think you know the reason I'm not so grumpy anymore, too."

"It wouldn't have anything to do with a certain young lady, would it?"

A smile exploded across Jim's face. "It sure wouldn't do any good for me to try to keep anything from you or Kay. You seem to catch on to everything."

"It didn't take a private detective to figure this one out."

Jim sprawled in an easy chair. "It is good to have things straightened out with Connie. I can tell you that much."

"We're happy for both of you," Kay told him.

"If you think there's a change in me, you should see the change in Connie. You'd scarcely know her. She's the way she used to be when we first started going together."

He went on to explain what had taken place and how the speaker had been able to help Connie see that God wasn't directing her to try to fill Fritz' responsibilities to Him.

"And now," he concluded, "she knows that God is only looking to her to do what He has called her to do, and she is actually doing far more for the Lord than before."

"That's wonderful," Kay murmured.

"She was so upset all the time she wasn't able to accomplish anything. Now things are straightened out and it's all different."

Danny nodded his understanding.

* * *

Jim had said nothing to anyone about going to see Johnny Larson. However, in the middle of the morning on Saturday, he drove to the garage where the boy worked and went in to talk to him. Johnny was hard at work when he approached him.

"Hi, Johnny," he said.

The other boy looked up, curiously. "Hi, Jim, I didn't know you were home." There was hesitation in his voice, as though he wanted to talk to the Bible school student and yet wasn't sure how he would be received.

"I just got in last night." He went over and leaned against a car. "Danny said you'd gotten a job out here."

Johnny paused momentarily. "Lester McCloud got it for me."

Jim already knew that, but he didn't tell Johnny that he did. "That was nice of him."

The younger boy's face twisted curiously. "I can't figure that guy out. If I were in his place, I'd be a lot different than he is, I'm afraid. I'd be more apt to want to get revenge."

"That's the way we are, naturally," Jim told him. "We want to hurt those who have hurt us. We want to get even with people – make them pay for their wrongdoing. But when Christ really gets hold of every phase of our lives, things are different. That's the reason Lester and Vivian McCloud have befriended you and have been trying to help you in every way they can."

Johnny glanced in the direction of the office. "I'd like to stand here and talk to you, Jim, but I'd better get back to work. I don't want somebody coming out here and firing me. This is the only place in town where I could get a job."

"I talked to Mr. Lohman on the way in," Jim said. "He said it would be all right if I took you out for a cup of coffee. How about it?"

The boy hesitated. "I was already out for coffee an hour or so ago."

"Mr. Lohman knows that, but he said it would be all right for you to go with me, if you'd like."

Johnny went to the front office, talked with his employer briefly and went in to wash up. Jim said no more to him until they were in the cafe over a cup of coffee, except to talk of general things like the weather and the condition of the snow for skiing. Once they were sitting across the table from each other, he changed the subject suddenly.

"How have things been going for you, Johnny?" he asked quietly.

The boy eyed him. "What do you mean?"

"I've been thinking a lot about you lately, Johnny," Jim went on. "How've you been making it?"

"All right, I guess."

Jim thought he detected a note of despondency in his companion's voice. "You don't sound as though it's been going too well."

Johnny managed a thin smile. "I guess I shouldn't have anything to complain about. At least I'm not in the reformatory, and that's more than I thought before the trial."

"Have you been getting to church and Sunday school regularly?"

Johnny nodded. "Haven't missed a Sunday."

"That's good." Jim stirred his coffee absent-mindedly. "When I first started living for the Lord, I found that I got more help in going to services regularly than just about anything I did, aside from reading my Bible and having a time of prayer every day."

Jim encouraged Johnny the best he knew how in the short time they had together before Johnny had to return to the garage.

When he got back to the Orlis home, he talked with Danny about the time he had spent with Johnny. "You know, Danny, we've got to try to find some Christian fellows who will take Johnny under their wing. The poor guy goes to school, goes home, goes to work, and on Sunday he goes to church, and that's about the size of it. He doesn't go anywhere with kids his own age."

Danny nodded. "This is something that has disturbed me a great deal, too. As nearly as I can find out, he doesn't have any friends."

"He's going to have plenty of trouble living for the Lord if that doesn't change. I know. I went through it myself."

* * *

Johnny went back to work with new vigor after talking with Jim that Saturday morning. It was sure something when a guy like that would come over and have coffee with him. And he didn't act as though he was ashamed to be seen with him, either. Jim was a great guy.

It was too bad he wasn't going to be in Fairview all the time. It would be good to have a fellow like him to go hunting and fishing with, or just to talk to when he was feeling sorry for himself. There were a lot of things he'd like to ask Jim about – things that he'd been reading in the Bible or heard the pastor bring up in his messages.

Johnny hadn't planned on asking anyone in his family to go to Sunday school and church with him the next morning. He had been wanting them to go and once in a while he had prayed for them, but most of the time he had been so discouraged he hadn't even prayed about it.

This particular Sunday morning, however, he felt better than he had for weeks. He got up at the usual time. His parents were still in bed. There wouldn't be any use in trying to get them to go with him, he knew, but Larry was another matter. He went in and wakened his younger brother.

"Hey! It's time for you to be getting up."

Larry rubbed his eyes, sleepily. "What for?" he asked. "This is Sunday, isn't it?"

"That's right. It's Sunday. And it's time for you to get up and go to Sunday school and church with me.

Larry stared at him. "You've got to be kidding."
"Come on. Get out of here, or I'll kick you out.

We haven't got all day."

Larry rolled over on his side. "I don't feel like going this morning, Johnny," he mumbled. "I'm tired."

"I'll fix breakfast while you're getting dressed."

The younger boy started to refuse again but changed his mind and got up. A few minutes later he went to the kitchen, still toying with his tie. "This is the earliest I've been up on a Sunday morning all year."

Johnny grinned. "It's not so bad when you get used to it."

Larry sat down, surveying the table critically. "One slice of burnt toast and some cold cereal. Big deal."

"I'll make a bargain with you. Next Sunday you fix breakfast. OK?"

Johnny asked the blessing and the two of them began to eat. It was several minutes before either spoke. Larry enjoyed being with his older brother, just the two of them.

"You know, Johnny," he said, "this is sort of fun, isn't it?"

Johnny grinned. "It sure is. And when you get started going to church, you'll find out you enjoy it even more than my wonderful breakfasts."

When Johnny and Larry came into church a few minutes later, Doug was standing in the foyer.

He saw them and beamed. "Hi, Johnny."

Johnny Larson's smile flickered. It was good to be

at church again. It was good to be among Christian people and with Christian friends. As he went and sat down a strange thought came to him, something he had never realized before. All of his old friends were gone. The only friends he had now were the Christians who wanted to help him. As he sat there, he prayed silently that God would help him to live in a way that would make them proud of him. After all they were doing for him, he couldn't let them down!

THE
DANNY ORLIS
SERIES

The Danny Orlis series, by Bernard Palmer, delivers a blend of adventure, mystery, and suspense through various settings—from the Canadian wilderness to Guatemalan jungles. Danny Orlis, an adept outdoorsman, skilled athlete, and committed Christian, employs his quick thinking, calm bravery, and biblical solutions to confront everyday problems and hair-raising dangers. Early stories focus on Danny navigating school life, sports, and outdoor challenges, while in later books, Danny and his wife Kay provide wisdom and guidance to youngsters facing lifelike situations and challenges. Having sold over two million copies, this series has made Palmer a renowned author in Christian youth literature. Palmer is also the author of the Felicia Cartright series and various other series for Christian youth.

AVAILABLE FROM WWW.ANEKOPRESS.COM

www.ingramcontent.com/pod-product-compliance
Lightning Source LLC
Chambersburg PA
CBHW060502300726
48975CB00008B/2610